I got so close I could smell the wolves' breath and see the flecks of color in their eyes. Very, very slowly, I knelt (do you know what it's like to look *up* at three very tense wolves?) and stretched my hands, palms up, on the ground in front of Tweedlioop.

For a few seconds he did nothing. Then, slowly, he crawled aboard and I lifted him, holding him close to my chest. The wolves watched closely, as if puzzled, but still did not move.

I didn't relax, nor did I slow up. On the contrary: I — *we* — made it out in two hours. The wolves were with us all the way. Every time I looked back, they were a little closer. Sometimes, if I stopped too long, the leader stepped forward and growled, as if determined to drive us out.

And I kept reflecting that they were just the beginning. Everything earthly would sense Tweedlioop's alienness.

STANLEY SCHMIDT

TWEEDLIOOP

A TOM DOHERTY ASSOCIATES BOOK

TWEEDLIOOP

Copyright © 1986 by Stanley Schmidt

First printing: November 1986
First mass-market printing: May 1988

A TOR Book

Published by Tom Doherty Associates, Inc.
49 West 24th Street
New York, NY 10010

ISBN: 0-812-53155-8
Can. No.: 0-812-53156-6

Printed in the United States of America

0 9 8 7 6 5 4 3 2 1

To Joyce
for being Joyce

1

THE SQUIRREL CAME RIGHT UP TO ME. HE STOPPED less than a yard away, shamelessly eyeing the nuts and candy and raisins I was mixing into gorp and packing into Ziploc bags for the next couple of days' lunches. I eyed him back, warily. "That's far enough."

The squirrel said nothing. My voice sounded out of place: alone down here at the end of the canyon, I hadn't heard one for hours. The quiet, unbroken except for the murmur of the river and the occasional purr of a passing seaplane, was—I hoped—what I needed. I didn't need pesky critters—even cute little red squirrels—trying to steal my food.

He inched closer with a deliberate stealth that somehow seemed wrong. I'm no zoologist, but I know squirrels move in quick little jerks and freeze between them to size things up. This guy just kept coming. "I warned you," I said. "Don't you understand English?" And I thought, *What's the big deal, anyway? Lots of animals act like this, where they haven't seen people or know they're protected. Even if he got it all, you could walk out to the road in three hours.*

The squirrel stopped, cocked his head, and stared up at me. Something was wrong with his right eye. "This is mine," I said. "You go find your own." He lowered his head and inched a little closer. "Shoo!" I yelled, swatting at him and carefully missing by inches.

He ignored me. I changed my tack. "Look," I said, picking up a handful of nuts and chocolates. "You can have this. Then get lost." I tossed it over the bank, down onto the rock and mud flat that edged the river. He watched curiously and then turned back to me. He glanced up, paused as if pondering, and then made a sudden, thoroughly squirrel-like dash straight toward the patch of moss and needles where I was sitting. He grabbed something and rebounded along the edge of the woods. Ten feet away he stopped, good eye fixed on me, and started chomping away like mad, on—

A Ziploc bag. My gorp—which the locals call "squirrel food," for painfully good reasons—was untouched, and that crazy critter was attacking that plastic bag as if it were the grandest feast in the world.

I laughed, relieved—but only for an instant. The whole purpose of putting food in those bags is to lock the smell in so the animals won't bother it. But if they develop a taste for the bags themselves . . .

Something, I thought, *is wrong with that squirrel.* I tried to look at him, to figure it out.

But he was gone, and so was my bag.

It kept bothering me all evening, though it had to compete for mind-space with a lot of other things. I was edgy, tense, overreacting to everything. I knew why, but I needed time to work it out. That was why I was here. Sam, my boss, had practically insisted I take a vacation, and this place—though Alaska had changed a lot since my last visit—still had a lot of what I needed.

I ate supper on the same patch where the squirrel with the eccentric tastes had robbed me. A shower was passing through, but the scraggly spruce of the taiga made a good enough canopy to keep me dry. No visitors came. I ate slowly, pensively, and then cleaned up and went down by the river. There was a rock there, patiently shaped and polished over the eons to serve as a sofa. It was cold and wet after the shower, but I spread my poncho on it and managed to get fairly comfortable. I did a little writing and a lot of thinking, and gradually a little of the accustomed tranquilizing effect began to work. The sky had cleared, and for a while I watched spectacular patterns of light and shadow on the cliffs up the canyon and the gentler tundra hills around me. Later I closed my eyes and listened to the river; I have no idea how long. When I opened them, some high cirrus clouds had appeared; down the river, beyond the silhouetted spruces on the left bank, they were painted red and gold by sunset. I watched it for a while, but in that country, in summer, sunsets develop so slowly that eventually you can tire of them. I gave up about ten o'clock, when it was pretty dusky, and started slowly back to my tent, tucked just inside one corner of the woods. I brushed aside a nagging thought that I was avoiding the things I needed to think about. *Don't rush me,* I countered. *Time's what I need. I can stay down here a week, if that's what it takes.*

A breeze stirred abruptly, fanning tree fragrance into my face. I was glad to be among them. They weren't much, but they had let me hang my food up, for what little protection that afforded. Normally I wouldn't have bothered; out on the tundra I would have had no choice. But after watching that squirrel, my confidence in plastic bags laid on the ground was badly shaken.

I was unzipping the mosquito netting on my tent when I heard the wolves. I stopped and sat up straight, listening. They weren't close—I could barely be sure they were real, over the rapids—and they were no threat in any case. But their howls—to a man with a lot on his mind, alone in a darkening wilderness thousands of miles from home—can be one of the most melancholy sounds you can imagine. Or maybe you can't.

I no longer felt like going to bed. Instead I felt a need for something cheering. I zipped the tent back up and went back down to the rocky shore to build a campfire. I couldn't remember whether it was allowed by my permit, but I didn't care. I needed it, and I'd make very sure it didn't hurt anything.

But it was a mistake anyway, and I should have known it. Everything I was trying to root gently out of my mind, those crackling orange flames stirred up again.

I was back in our house, the night it happened. Kit's Castle, I called it, because it was she who'd spotted it and made me stop the car. She loved it; I liked it; the new boom in space made it possible, and we moved in within three weeks. Not that I was complaining. It was a nice place, old, a sort of miniature Georgian mansion with an acre of lush subtropical greenery, and only a half hour from the plant.

A cold front had arrived that night, and almost chilly breezes played through the open bedroom windows, whipping the curtains around. Kit and I loved it, after two weeks of heat wave, but Les, the four-year-old, had a cold and Kit worried about him. We'd shut off the lights and were lying together, letting the breeze tickle us while our eyes adapted and let us see stars through the window. Just when I was getting very comfortable, Kit said, "This may be too much for Les. Maybe I should check."

I talked her out of it. But a little later his thin voice drifted along the hallway to us. "Mommy, I can't sleep."

Kit was always a pushover. I didn't try to stop her, but I was so close to sleep I had to make a conscious effort to stay awake until she got back. I watched her disappear along the hall she liked so much—mirrors along one side, glass doors opening onto the balcony on the other—with no light except the tiny green night-light Les insisted on. I listened to their voices, his anxious and hers reassuring, and felt a warm, fuzzy sense of being very lucky. I drifted down closer to sleep, and the snatches of talk drifted farther away. "I'll start a vaporizer," Kit said. "That'll help you breathe." Sounds of puttering. Footsteps. The bathroom light off the mirror side of the hall came on briefly. Darkness returned. Kit's voice, again from Les's room, then his.

"No. Don't close the door."

I heard her stop with it half closed. "I have to, Les. You need to breathe, and—"

A gust rattled window frames and Les's door blew shut, cutting off the voices. I became dimly aware that the silence was lasting too long, but I knew Les could be hard to reason with. But then came a rattling, a more and more frenzied shaking of Les's door, as if Kit couldn't open it. I frowned and thought distantly of turning on a light and going to help. Kit's muffled voice came through the door. "Bill, can you get this? It's stuck."

"Coming." I gathered my thoughts enough to remember how to get out of bed. I didn't bother with the light.

"I think the lock's jammed," said the muffled Kit. "I'll bet Les stuck something in—"

And then the scream. How am I ever going to forget that? Or the way it turned into, *"Fire!"*? Or the glow from around the corner that I wasn't sure was real until it burst forth in a roaring orange blaze?

The door was glass; everything in that hall was glass. Suddenly Kit was gone, and then she was back, silhouetted against the heavy panes, with Les in her arms. He was screaming; she was pounding and yelling something about time.

For a little while I stood petrified at the far end of the hall. How long, I don't know, but it couldn't have been very long and yet it was too long. I struggled to get my brain revved up, just as I used to struggle to start my car on winter mornings when we lived up north. Adrenaline helped, but even that was slow in coming. I'd half-expected Kit would break the glass, but those panes were rugged, and the small-celled frame that held them even more so. I'd need a tool. . . .

Coming awake, I ducked back into our bedroom, yanked a drawer out of the dresser, and dumped the contents on the floor. Running down the hall with that as a battering ram, I might get through. I hoped they'd still have room to stand aside when the door broke.

And then we could all run back and go out our bedroom window to the cedars below.

But when I got back to the door, Kit and Les were

huddled all the way over by the outside wall, yelling frantically, and the hall was filled with flame. I was too late . . .

Or was I? Were the flames in the hall real, or just a trick of all that glass?

I stood like an idiot or a drunk, trying to decide. Wheels turned sluggishly in my brain. Could I get through or not?

The few seconds that I pondered were all it took. Fanned by a gust from a window Kit had missed, the flames swelled to fill the room.

And *then,* unmistakably, they broke through, and I knew that the hall had been safe. I could have done it. But everything was ablaze and even the silhouettes of my wife and boy were gone.

Now it *was* too late. There was nothing to do except get myself back as fast as possible and out that window.

I spent the rest of the night thinking of all the ways I should have known. The shadows of the slats that kept Kit from breaking through, the framework that supported the hallway mirrors . . .

But those are little, subtle things. I can't really be blamed for not seeing them clearly, as groggy as I was. Can I?

The investigation showed everything. Those guys are good, and Kit's Castle was rugged enough to save some clues. Les *had* jammed something in the lock; four-year-olds do things like that. And some faulty wiring had started the fire when Kit plugged in the vaporizer.

They even figured out how it had spread, and how much time there'd been when I could have got them out. They were gentle; nobody said—to my face—that I should have done anything I didn't. But I heard the gossip. *He didn't do anything,* they whispered. *He didn't even try.*

I knew they were wrong, but gradually I began to believe them. Months after the grief should have been largely healed, I was still brooding—and it was getting worse rather than better. Eventually it got so bad that Sam took me aside one day and said, in entirely too fatherly a way, "Bill, why don't you take some vacation early this year?"

I objected; I said I couldn't enjoy it. He looked straight at me and said sadly, "I know. I'm not talking about enjoyment."

In the end I gave in. Sam kept after me, and I finally admitted that going way, way off by myself might be just what I needed.

But it wasn't working. Annoyed, I scrubbed out the fire and brought water from the river in one of my cooking pans and doused it until the coals were as cold as the night.

But I couldn't put out the memories the fire had reawakened. They followed me back to my tent and gave me no real rest until long past midnight.

I can't exactly say it dawned bright and clear. In that season and place, dawns are no better defined than sunsets, and besides, I slept through it. But it was bright and clear when I finally woke up, around ten-thirty, and that helped me feel better. I remembered enough of last night's doubts to provoke halfhearted thoughts about whether to pack back out today or to stick it out awhile longer. But I felt refreshed enough by my sleep, and my amorphous approximation of a western omelet tasted good enough, and the day seemed nice enough, that when I finished eating I was in no hurry to leave.

I let my mind settle back for a very relaxing day. I finished eating unhurriedly, letting my eyes almost focus on the dancing sparkles of the rapids twenty yards away.

As I was scraping the last scraps out of the bowl, a dart of motion off to one side caught my eye. A squirrel—but not the same one that had ignored my food and swiped the wrapper yesterday. This one had two good eyes. Feeling somehow relieved, I scraped the last bit of food out onto the ground and watched amiably as he gathered it up, a yard from my knee.

But as I watched, some of yesterday's uneasiness returned, for a different reason. There was *nothing* unnerving about this fellow. He looked and acted exactly the way a squirrel should.

And that brought back, more intensely, yesterday's vague hunch that the other one didn't. That there was something *wrong* with the other one, and I mean something more wrong than a bad eye.

I heard a rustle, and the squirrel I was watching stiffened warily. I followed his gaze. Yesterday's squirrel had reappeared, and the two of them were staring at each other, momentarily ignoring me. Glancing back and forth between them, I grew more conscious of their differences. The strange one was too brown—and all over, not just on top. His tail was too short and stiff, his head too big. His one good eye had a long elliptical pupil, while the "normal" one's were big and round. His hands . . .

Hands?

With a sudden ratchet-burst of scolding, the normal one turned and dashed headlong into the woods. His voice faded, and I looked back at the other. The morning no longer seemed so clear. I looked hard, and shivered slightly as I caught myself thinking, *That's not a squirrel.*

Had that bit about the hands been overactive imagination? I stared hard at his tiny forepaws, but I couldn't decide. My eyes wandered back to his face. He stared back at me with a fixed, unsquirrel-like expression. He looked tired, I thought, and unhealthy. We must have looked at each other for a full minute, I trying to figure out what to make of him, he trying to figure . . .

Who knows?

On an impulse born of curiosity and compassion, I tossed him another Ziploc bag and a couple of nuts. He came forward, more slowly than yesterday, and took the bag. Ignoring the nuts, he dragged the bag off—this time slowly, and only a few feet—and started eating. This time there was no hurry, but my impression was of listlessness rather than confidence.

He's sick, I decided.

He finished the bag and we kept staring at each other. I couldn't decide what I thought or felt about the whole situation, but I was sure now that he wasn't a squirrel.

I hadn't figured out what he *was* when he opened his mouth (it opened oddly, somehow), looked me straight in the eye, and said, "Tweedlioop."

Not really, of course. But it sounded enough like that to register that way in my mind—a soft, liquid utterance that could never come from an ordinary squirrel. Some kind of bird, maybe, but not a squirrel.

And I was sure this was no bird.

"Tweedlioop," I mimicked. "As good a name as any. And I'm Bill Nordstrom. You talk?"

He made more liquid noises, and for an instant I could almost believe he really was talking. But then he started darting around, quite normally, and I relaxed a little. Of course he was a squirrel; he just had a few quirks. So does my brother-in-law. If these wild imaginings were what holing up in the wilderness did for me, maybe I'd better reconsider its medicinal value.

Between dashes he'd stop and look at me and chatter. After a while it dawned on me that his dashes followed a definite pattern, and I began to recognize sequences in his chatterings. Some of the uneasiness returned. *He's trying to tell me something,* I thought, and immediately tried to shake the thought off.

But he kept it up. He'd run toward me, chatter, turn and run toward the edge of the bank, stop and look back at me, and chatter some more. Then he'd wait a few seconds and do it all again. His tail dragged stiffly behind him. His runs toward me came closer, and when he stopped he'd look up and wave with his oddly shaped front paw. Then I noticed that the other end of his run was always at the top of the little path I used to go down to the river.

"You want me to follow you?" Tentatively, and feeling a little ridiculous, I stood up. Tweedlioop paused at my feet and watched, tilting his head back. As soon as I was up, he turned and darted away, gurgling excitedly. He stopped at the top of the path, but only long enough to make sure I was following.

Then he darted down the path.

Well, I thought, *I was right about that.* But the thought that he was intelligent didn't come yet. I used to have a cat who told me where to go, too, but she wasn't too smart otherwise.

Down by the river, he stopped beside a rock-free expanse of smooth gray mud the size of a garbage-can lid.

He waited till I caught up, then started scratching something in the mud with a forepaw. I sat down on a rock to watch. It started to look like a rifle target, with a tiny circle in the middle and half a dozen larger ones surrounding it, all nice and neat. Not very big, of course; Tweedlioop wasn't very big, and he took great pains to keep stray paw prints out of his work area. But they were amazingly symmetrical.

Lifting one muddy paw, he gestured at the small central circle, then at the sun in the sky, then at the central circle . . .

"Good Lord!" I breathed, my mind grinding gears as it shifted into high.

Tweedlioop licked the mud off his paw and I decided it *was* a hand. Three chubby little fingers and two tiny thumbs, but more hand than paw. Watching me intently, he pointed at the second circle around his "sun," then gestured broadly around us, at the hills and woods and river and sky, then back at the second circle.

The *second* circle?

Well, nobody's perfect. How many humans know what orbit they're in? How many airline passengers really read up on their destinations before they go?

He chirped and twittered, then ran way off toward the river, on the opposite side of the open mud circle. Everything he'd drawn so far had been on the near side, but now he came charging toward me, straight across the circle, leaving a clear line of vaguely wrong-looking tracks.

Which bent smoothly into a much larger circle, extending beyond his mud and onto the rocks, neatly encircling his solar system. He ran around it two or three times, exactly retracing his path, then stopped and leaned back on his tail as if pondering. Neither of us moved or made any sound, and I became very conscious of the soothing white roar of the rapids.

Eventually another sound emerged: the drone of a plane. I looked up; so did Tweedlioop. A green and white Cessna seaplane appeared over the edge of the woods and passed directly over, climbing and veering up the canyon to the south. Just before it disappeared, Tweedlioop jabbed his paw toward it, jabbering torrentially. He started racing around that circle again, then stopped, pointed again toward the fast-fading noise of the plane, and stared at me. He was shaking, almost too fast to see.

"Okay," I said. "Take it easy. I read you, I think. Something flew you here and parked out past the planets. Or some of them. Then what?"

Very gradually, he stopped shaking. Leaning back on his tail, he lifted both hands to his chest. He pointed at the sky, and then at his feet, and traced a line in the mud from himself to the point he'd already indicated was Earth.

I had the picture, but I was too numb to try to reply in any meaningful way. I was still struggling to get over thinking of him as a squirrel. He didn't even look like one, on close inspection, but the coincidental resemblance was close enough to fool a lot of uninitiated humans.

The systems engineer in me marveled dispassionately at his compactness, trying to imagine how his evolution had managed to cram that kind of intelligence into that kind of body. But most of me was speculating—not nearly so dispassionately—on what advantages their appearance could give them in an invasion.

And all the questions that led to.

Finally I managed, "Where are the others?" My throat felt dry and tight.

It was stupid, anyway. He could no more understand my vocalizations than I could understand his. (Or could he?) He may have been trying to tell me that with his new gesticulations, but I got nothing from them but a sense of frustration fed by urgency. After a few minutes he gave up and slunk off, listless as when I first saw him this morning, toward the sheltering woods.

And I headed for my sofa rock, deep in thought. I ought, it seemed to me, to be doing something. But what?

I wasn't even sure what the problem was.

I had some idea, of course, but it took an effort to think about it. The notion of an army of cute little squirrels waiting out past Pluto to do something to Earth was hard to take seriously. Thinking of Tweedlioop as sinister and dangerous was next to impossible.

But I had to. Tweedlioop was here, he was intelligent, and I could think of no more plausible explanation than he had given me. He had come from the stars. A race that could do that, by definition, had abilities that we could not view lightly until we knew far more about their aims.

I had to find out. Where were the others? What were they doing here? Why? How?

I would have to ask Tweedlioop, presumably by scratching things in the mud.

But . . . if it *was* an invasion, would he tell me?

Maybe I'd have to trick him. And that bothered me. Damn it, he didn't *look* like an invader.

I pondered through lunch without seeing a sign of him. But when I finished hanging my food bag back up, I turned around and there he was, at my feet, looking up.

He looked terrible. He dragged himself across the ground; he drooped. And that reminded me that he had a problem too. He was sick, and alone, and a long way from home.

Briefly, sympathy threatened to wash away the suspicion I had to feel. He was looking at my dangling red food sack. I let it down enough to fish out a Ziploc bag. He crawled to it and ate it where it lay. I pondered his craving for them, and realized that he must find it hard to get a suitable diet here, if his story was true. The bag must provide some vital nutrient that the tundra and taiga couldn't. . . .

He finished the bag and started away. After a few yards, he stopped and looked back as if to see whether I was following. Seeing that I wasn't, he came back to me, turned away, and looked back again. I started walking, and he kept going.

He led me back to the river, to his picture. With no preliminaries, he started around the distant orbit where I gathered the starship had parked. After a few quick circuits, he turned inward along the line that led to Earth. Halfway in, he swayed back on his tail, swinging his hands skyward, then swinging the right one parallel to the ground, just like Les imitating an airplane.

Except Tweedlioop's plane crashed. His hand fell abruptly and he went sprawling in the mud.

He started repeating, but I already understood. "Where?" I asked aloud. But this time, instead of wasting time feeling foolish, I immediately followed the spoken question with a sweeping gesture around us and a questioning shrug. He showed no recognizable sign of understanding, so I tried variations.

And felt definite satisfaction as he lifted one small arm to point steadily up and southwest.

The hill beyond our woods? Beyond it? How far?

Here was something I might be able to check. But as I struggled to find a way to ask, Tweedlioop dropped his Statue-of-Liberty pose and started something new. He pointed to himself, retraced the line to the parking orbit, then stopped and pointed to himself.

And then to me, with a long look that conveyed pleading with astonishing clarity across all the alienness that separated us. It took several repetitions before I thought I had it—partly because I couldn't believe it at first.

He wanted me to help him get back to the mother ship?

"Ridiculous!" I snorted when it hit me. Even if it was true, and they posed no threat, what could I do? I shrugged helplessly. "Sorry," I said. "I'd like to help, but no can do." I thought a little and remembered a question that was as pertinent to him as to us. I knelt beside the mud, pointed straight at Tweedlioop, and made a questioning gesture around as if looking for others like him.

He didn't understand. I couldn't blame him. It was a lousy attempt.

I tried again. With a fingertip, I traced what was supposed to be a picture of him. It was pretty crude, so when it was finished I pointed at it, then at him. Then I drew three more.

He stared at it for a long time, then lay down, sprawled on his stomach.

Dead? The others were dead?

Suddenly he was on his feet again, tugging at my pants

cuff and making those little dashes and over-the-shoulder looks that said to follow him.

But this time I hesitated. Where did he want to take me? Up the hill? To see the remains?

Did I want to do that?

For a goodly while I hesitated, memories of my indecision that other night flickering through my mind. In the end curiosity won out. I went with him, and this time he went at a pace that was hard to match.

Around the brushy corner of the woods we went, and up the open tundra hill to the southwest. Spongy soil carpeted with lichens and tiny flowers gave underfoot. Mosquitoes swarmed around us; a couple of planes passed nearby. My heart pounded with the effort to keep up. Tweedlioop splashed through a couple of rivulets; I jumped them. In minutes, our little patch of forest sprawled below us, the first of several dark green beads strung along the Savage, against a backdrop of gentler hills and big sky.

Tweedlioop topped a small ridge, led me down it, then dropped down the far side where a shallow gully fanned out onto almost level ground. I caught a smell, powerful but utterly unfamiliar . . .

And there it was.

I drew my breath in sharply, skidding to a halt with my eyes riveted to the wreckage before me. It was so *tiny!* It was hardly more than a big can, no bigger than a VW Beetle, made of something that first looked like orange plastic but then showed the faintest of metallic gleams.

The engineer in me struggled to imagine what could have powered such a thing in interplanetary flight. The rest of me stared at the ugly, crumpled gash down its side. The smell was coming from there.

I glanced at Tweedlioop, feeling awkward. He came toward me, touched the toe of my boot, and continued to the wreck, bracing himself against the hull, reaching up as high toward the split as he could. I bent down next to him. The smell grew strong, almost dizzying. The ground here was even spongier; a tiny streamlet flowed right under the shuttle, gurgling faintly. I looked again at Tweedlioop, then leaned forward and made myself look inside.

I hadn't brought a flashlight, but the sun was still high, and I could make out forms inside. Not instruments. Bodies—sprawling, barely beginning to decompose, smeared here and there with something caked and brown. One vaguely resembled a wolverine with long orange fur and a vestigial tail; another, just as vaguely, a large, greenish-tinged marmot. Still small, for intelligent adults, but not as absurdly so as Tweedlioop.

And now I understood. Tweedlioop was just a kid. A young, lost, helpless kid who for some reason had been roaming the stars with his family and had been orphaned in an alien wilderness.

I reached out automatically to touch him, gently stroking his fur. It felt like felt, but springy. He didn't object. I realized gradually that mosquitoes were buzzing all around me, and some had attacked. My repellent was back at camp. It didn't matter.

I looked back in the shuttle. One more body—like Tweedlioop but a little larger and considerably greener—lay wedged in an opening to an inner compartment, an opening through which Tweedlioop could barely have squeezed.

For a long time we knelt like that. My thoughts were

darting every which way, but I sensed that somewhere among them was one that knew where it wanted to go and was struggling to break through the confusion. Finally it did.

If Tweedlioop was what he seemed, maybe he did just want what he said. And maybe I *could* help. Not me, personally—but NASA, my company, or both. Now that space is opening up again, and industry's starting to move out, there are big things afoot. I've caught enough rumors at work to suspect there just might be something in the works that could help him back to his ship.

If anybody influential thought it was worthwhile—and safe. Big ifs. The whole thing was, at best, an extreme long shot. And it would take a long time, even if it could be done.

And if I asked, a whole hornet's nest of bureaucrats would descend on my little lost kid, asking all the questions I'd asked earlier, checking the worst assumptions they could imagine about his origins and intentions. They'd argue about whose jurisdiction he fell under, whether he should be helped or exterminated. . . .

And through it all he'd be helpless, while quite likely most of his life ticked futilely away. It would be hell for him. And they might decide the wrong thing.

I couldn't blame them. Sure, they'd have to ask all those questions.

But did I have to expose him to all that, almost surely for nothing? It might be worth it, if there was really any chance. But when I tried to look at it realistically, the chance I could see was so infinitesimal it hardly seemed worth seeking. He might be better off just staying here. He'd survived so far, hadn't he?

It was the hardest decision I'd ever made, but I made

it. Taking him back, opening that can of worms, keeping him in suspense for years, and then finding that his ship had left while we argued—that would be no favor.

I couldn't look at him as I stood up. "Sorry," I grunted, with a helpless shrug I thought he'd recognize. "Still can't help."

I took off down the hill, walking fast for camp. I thought I heard him following me, but I didn't look back.

I slept even worse that night. It clouded over, and it was late enough in the season that it got almost dark. The winds came up during the night and howled and moaned and whipped the trees about so I wondered how I was going to take the tent down in the morning.

For I would take it down. I was leaving. That decision was made.

The other, that I thought I had made on the hill, would not lie still. It haunted me all night. I kept thinking of new angles. Mightn't Tweedlioop's people send another shuttle down to look for survivors, when his group failed to return? Would they have any hope of finding him if they did?

How would they react if they found we were holding him and making our own decisions about him?

Was leaving him here really the lesser evil?

My dreams, whenever I got close to sleep, flared up in flames, with silhouettes of window slats and Kit and Les. And Tweedlioop.

And echoes of not-quite-heard voices. *He didn't do anything. He didn't even try.*

In the morning I lay in my sleeping bag, watching the trees raking the gloomy sky, wishing the wind would die.

Sometimes I thought it was going to; then I decided that, if anything, it was getting worse. I'd better get up and out while I could. It wouldn't be easy now, but it might be worse later.

It wasn't as bad as I thought, once I got outside. The noise was mostly the wind breaking against treetops and fringes, so most of the force was spent when it reached my tent. I'd do all right, using rocks to hold the tent corners down while I pulled stakes.

Tweedlioop was waiting just outside. I suspected he'd been there all night. He looked at me, even his good eye looking dull, but he didn't try to tell me anything. I avoided his gaze as I went for my food and stove.

The stove wouldn't work right: the wind was too strong and variable, and it's temperamental even when things are good. Tweedlioop lay on his stomach on a bed of spruce needles, watching me fiddle with it until I gave up, put it away, and resigned myself to a bag of gorp.

Then he lifted his head and twittered like crazy. *The bag,* I thought. *Okay. It's the least I can do.* I dumped it in my lap and tossed him the bag. He ate it without getting up from where he lay.

I felt uncomfortable, eager to be on my way. As soon as I finished eating, I stood up and started stuffing everything into my pack. I started to put the food sack in and stopped halfway. If I was leaving, what did I need with it? Tweedlioop apparently needed something in the plastic. He was welcome to those, and whatever else he could use. "Here," I said, dumping the whole thing on the ground in front of him. "My compliments and best wishes."

A voice inside me called me names I don't care to

remember. But I knew it would be doing that no matter what I did.

I went back to take the tent down and lash it and the sleeping bag to my pack. Tweedlioop followed me, but I tried to pretend he wasn't there.

When it was done, I got a tree to help me on with the pack. "Good-bye, Tweedlioop," I said. "Good luck." And I found the faint trace of a trail that led out of the woods and started up the canyon.

I must have gone a quarter mile before that voice inside me made me listen. *Who are you kidding?* it demanded, shaking me by my mental lapels. *A few scraps of food and plastic. How long will that last him. A week?*

Face it. You saw how he needs those bags. Whatever he needs, he can't get here without them. When the few you left are gone, he's finished.

If you take him out and try to help him . . . yes, he'll suffer. Maybe he'll die. Probably you'll fail.

Leave him here . . . he will *die. Period. Soon.*

And you still don't know what to do?

I stopped. Slowly, I turned and started back. But I reached the edge of the taiga running, as well as I could with the pack, and shouting, "Tweedlioop!"

And stopped in my tracks, convulsed by a chill that shot up my backbone, exploded through the rest of my body, and wouldn't stop.

He was lying right where I'd left him—but around him paced three wolves, tails slightly raised, eyeing him intently. They were the ones I'd heard two nights ago, I guessed, the day I met Tweedlioop. Then I'd dismissed them as no threat—and normally I would have been right. They won't bother humans, under any normal circumstances.

But Tweedlioop wasn't human. He was something not of Earth, with an alien chemistry. Even I had sensed that. How much more obvious must it be to these creatures— virtually my siblings compared to Tweedlioop, but with vastly more sensitive noses? What must they have felt when they caught his scent, and the stronger ones of alien death from his crashed shuttle? Fear, I imagined, and curiosity. Should something so alien be avoided or investigated? Evidently curiosity had won out. Now they were here to face the threat, warily circling and eyeing and sniffing an animal that they could have eaten in one bite.

They were edgy, and now I was included in their edginess. And it was pretty obvious I couldn't count on them to behave normally.

Okay, I thought. *What now, little man? It was easy when all you had to do was pick him up and leave the real decisions for later. Can you still do it when* they're *here?*

They were twenty feet from me, and they were still paying more attention to Tweedlioop than to me. If I started backing up, slowly, right now, they'd probably let me leave. I could get out safely.

But Tweedlioop wouldn't last five minutes.

I could hear those voices again, louder than ever. And I knew that if I did the only thing that was obviously sane, they'd never stop.

Slowly, wishing I could remember more about even *normal* wolf behavior, I edged forward. I talked to them, quietly; I remembered that griz sometimes found that soothing, and maybe these guys would like it, too. "Easy," I said, hoping they could hear me over the pounding of my heart. "He's not going to hurt you. I'm not, either. Let me take him away, and you'll never see either of us again."

Their tails rose a little more, stiffening, at my first step forward. A trio of low growls rose from their throats. Somehow I kept going, very slowly, very steadily. Two of them kept their eyes on Tweedlioop. The third, his tail held higher than theirs, glared steadfastly at me. But none of them moved. A little piece of my mind observed with oddly cool detachment that each step I took was increasingly likely to be my last, and that Tweedlioop would be no better off for my efforts.

But I kept taking them.

I got so close I could smell the wolves' breath and see the flecks of color in their eyes. Very, very slowly, I knelt (do you know what it's like to look *up* at three very tense wolves?) and stretched my hands, palms up, on the ground in front of Tweedlioop.

For a few seconds he did nothing. Then, slowly, he crawled aboard and I lifted him, holding him close to my chest. The wolves watched closely, as if puzzled, but still did not move.

I turned and started out. Were they following me? I had to assume they were, but I didn't dare to look back until I reached the point where I had earlier turned around to come back.

They were still there. Not so close—maybe fifty feet back—but following with an air of patient determination that said, "It doesn't matter when we strike. We can get you whenever we like."

They could, too.

I didn't relax, nor did I slow up. On the contrary: I—*we*—made it out in two hours. The wolves were with us all the way. Every time I looked back, they were a little closer. Sometimes, if I stopped too long, the leader stepped forward and growled, as if determined to drive us out.

And I kept reflecting that they were just the beginning. Everything earthly would sense Tweedlioop's alienness. I wondered if I should try to tell him what he'd be up against even if I got him out, and how little he could hope for. But I gave it up. It was too complicated. He was a smart kid, anyway. He knew.

I half expected the wolves to leave us when we came in sight of the road, where the trail ran clear across open land. They didn't, and that unnerved me more than anything yet. They stayed right with me, now close as dogs at heel, driving me ever harder.

I kept going. The bridge looked so close, now; I hoped I would live to set foot on it. The sun was well up, and I was much too warm, but I hadn't dared stop to shed any layers. Everything I wore was drenched with sweat.

I reached the bridge. The wolves crossed the road with me, and I was struck by the question: who would stop for me when I was surrounded by wolves?

I ducked behind some alders and was ironically relieved when they followed. That should keep them out of sight when a vehicle approached, and then maybe I could make a dash for it and get inside before they could react.

Sure. Maybe I'd get *really* lucky and the vehicle would finally scare them off.

I kept my pack on and sat on a rock to wait, stroking Tweedlioop and talking softly to calm him and the wolves —and myself. I don't remember what I said—the words don't matter—but Tweedlioop seemed to be listening. The wolves sat on their haunches, looking warily at Tweedlioop, occasionally licking their lips with long tongues.

Finally, yellow flashed around a distant bend, one of the school buses pressed into shuttle service along the gravel road, now headed out toward the nearest outpost of civilization. I stood up, very deliberately, but made myself wait until the last minute before stepping out of the bushes. I also decided I'd better tuck Tweedlioop out of sight in the big zipper pocket in the front of my parka. "For your own good," I told him.

He didn't object, but the wolves rose and edged closer, with menacing noises and tail gestures. For a second I thought I'd finally driven them over the line, but again they stopped just short of attack. My heart was pounding as the bus pulled up and I made my move, stepping boldly out into the driver's sight. To my great relief, the wolves hesitated slightly, and the driver braked smoothly if noisily to a halt right in front of me. He started to open the door—

And the wolves made their move.

As if belatedly recognizing their last chance, they bounded around the bushes, releasing all their pent-up energy and fear in an explosion of furious yapping. All three jumped up on me, almost knocking me down, clawing and snapping at Tweedlioop's hiding place. I glimpsed astonishment and horror on the bus driver's face; the door slammed shut. I yelled and pounded on it with one hand while trying to push wolves away with the other. They dragged me down and tore my clothes and drew blood in several places, but I would have fared far worse if they'd really been after *me*. As it was, I hardly had time to notice the pain and the blood; it was only later that I realized that Tweedlioop stayed quiet through the whole thing. Somehow I kept them away from him, but I wasn't sure how long that could last.

I was dimly aware of shouts aboard the bus, and then

a crash of shattering glass and people jumping out windows. Suddenly there were two extra men in the fray, jabbing with ice axes and swinging them sideways. "Open up!" one of them yelled. And then, to me, "Get aboard! We'll be right behind you!"

The driver still looked uncertain, but the door swung open and I staggered through it, pack and all, while the two climbers kept the wolves busy. Abruptly, unexpectedly, all three animals wheeled and streaked away toward the nearest patch of taiga. The climbers jumped aboard, their axes lightly touched with blood, and the bus lurched forward. It was well on its way before the door was closed.

It was less than half full, and all the passengers crowded around me. Their voices were a numbing chorus:

"Are you all right?"

"Never saw anything like it!"

And so on.

I didn't have enough left to face it. Not now. "I'm fine," I lied. I turned to my rescuers. "How about you? I sure appreciate—"

"We're okay," one of them said. "What got into them? Attacking you right out here by the road, and then just quitting and running off like that—"

I knew, of course, but I was in no mood to explain. "Beats me." Clutching the Tweedlioop pocket protectively, I groped along the aisle toward the back of the bus.

"But you're bleeding," a woman said.

"I know. I'll live. Please—just leave me alone. I'll be okay."

They all looked after me peculiarly, but they respected my wishes and didn't follow me. I stumbled to the rearmost seat and flopped down in it. I was drained, and not yet ready to throw Tweedlioop to the *human* wolves.

But I was ready to face them now, when the time came. The voices in the front of the bus buzzed on, but *my* voices had stopped. Slouching down behind the seat in front of me, I unzipped Tweedlioop's pocket to sneak a peek. He was okay—or at least no worse than he had been.

And I, I suddenly realized, felt far better than anybody should who'd just been through what I had.

I looked at the tiny face peering out at me and grinned. Somehow the stars no longer seemed so far away—for either of us.

"We'll show 'em," I whispered, patting his head.

And for the first time, I dared to believe it.

II

EVEN WITH SEVERAL STOPS FOR GAWKING AT WILD-
life it only took a half hour to reach Morino. I got off at
the first handy spot, where an unmarked path headed
through woods to the campground.

The driver, a slim young man with long sandy hair who
I guessed to be a college student, didn't open the door
right away. "You ought to report that thing with the
wolves," he told me.

"I know. I will."

He still didn't open the door. There were other people
waiting in the aisle. "I'm supposed to make sure you do,"
the driver said. "Those wolves could be rabid. They've
certainly been hurt by humans, and that could turn them
dangerous. The rangers will want to check it out. Why
don't you stay on and let me run you over to the station?"

"I'd rather wait," I said, beginning to get annoyed. "I
want to claim a campsite and get set up and rest a little
first. Okay?"

"Well . . ."

"Look," said somebody behind me, "he's right. A little
rest and first aid before filling out forms. I'll see that he
does it."

I turned, frowning. Who was this stranger taking it upon herself to make promises on my behalf?

It was the woman who had commented that I was bleeding as I staggered to the back of the bus. She was tiny —five feet even, I guessed—but didn't look as though she needed any protection. She had long reddish-brown hair and bright green eyes and she spoke before I could. "Paul's right," she told me. "You have to report the wolves, for other people's safety if not your own. But you could use a little patching-up first. I'd be glad to do it for you. I'm good at it."

I found myself staring at her, forgetting what I was going to say about minding her own business. The last thing I needed now was to get mixed up with a stranger, and I like to think I'm too rational to trust people because they *look* trustworthy. But some of the people you meet out here are like that, and what came out of my mouth was, "Well . . . okay. Thanks."

The driver still looked doubtful, but he said, "I guess that'll be all right. Good luck, mister. Hope the rest of your stay's better."

He opened the door. And I found myself standing on a gravel path watching a yellow school bus pull away, with an alien hidden in my coat and having just entrusted myself to the care of a girl in her late twenties whom I'd never seen before in my life. "Doesn't look like you have any trouble walking," she said. "C'mon. My tent's not far."

I walked along beside her, fascinated by the way she'd stepped into my life and simultaneously trying to think of how to disengage myself while Tweedlioop was still my secret. She babbled happily on. "My name's Danni.

Danette O'Millian, actually, but nobody's saddled me with all that since I left the Lower Forty-eight."

I didn't volunteer my name and she didn't ask for it. "Thanks for helping me off the bus," I said. "I appreciate that. But I can take care of myself; no need to burden you. I ought to go make camp."

We had emerged into the campground, and Danni stopped and looked at me. Morino's a nice one: an open grove of aspens with space for a couple of dozen small tents, near the railroad tracks; and since it serves mostly as a way station for backpackers between trips, it attracts a nice clientele.

Danni seemed to see through me more easily than I'd hoped. "You seem anxious to get away," she said. "Is something wrong? Aside from being mauled by wolves."

"No. . . ."

"Then bear with me a few more minutes. You have no business pitching a tent until you're sure all your bleeding's under control, at least."

Again I gave in and followed her, against what remained of my better judgment. Her tent, set in a small clearing near the edge of the grove and well away from any others, looked too large for her. It was a freestanding dome of red nylon, of the size advertised "for two or three persons." Not cheap. "This is it," she said with a wave of her hand. "Hang up your coat and we'll see what we can do for you."

I leaned my pack against a tree, then took off my parka and hung it very carefully on a stub of an aspen branch. What I wanted more than anything else was to get away by myself where I could give Tweedlioop some fresh air and see how he was doing. Well, Danni's campsite was fairly secluded, anyway. . . .

But as she knelt to unzip her tent door, I heard her say, "Laurie?"

And a sleepy voice from inside said, "Hi, Mommy. Have a nice trip?"

Oh, no, I groaned silently. *You didn't tell me you had a kid.*

Danni ducked into the tent and popped out with first-aid kit in hand, closely followed by an eight- or nine-year-old girl with blond bangs and freckles. "My daughter Laurie," Danni told me. "She wanted to go on a guided walk this morning and then loaf around here. Laurie, this is . . ." She smiled sheepishly. "May we ask?"

"Sure," I said. "Bill. Hi, Laurie."

"Hi."

"Bill had a little problem with some wolves," Danni explained. "I offered him some bandages. Bill, why don't you sit there?" She indicated one of the few respectable-sized rocks on the ground. I sat down down and leaned back against a trunk, delivering myself into her care. She worked deftly, rolling up sleeves and loosening clothes where necessary, swabbing and examining and bandaging so expertly that I wondered if she was a nurse. Laurie sat cross-legged in the door of the tent, watching with wide-eyed curiosity.

"I thought wolves didn't bother people," Laurie said.

"They don't," I said, "normally."

"So why did these? Did you try to *feed* them or something?"

"Oh, no. I know better than that."

"We really don't know," Danni said. "Animals can be

unpredictable. That's why I always tell you to give them lots of room." I could tell she shared Laurie's suspicions that I had done something wrong. But she finished the last bandage and flashed me a nice professional smile as she rolled my pants leg down over my boot. "You got off pretty easy," she told me. "Just scratches, mainly. I don't think you'll have any problem—but be sure the rangers know how to reach you in case there *was* something wrong with those pups."

"Thanks," I said. "I was pretty lucky running into you, too. Could hardly count on the first person I ran into being a nurse."

Danni laughed cheerfully. "Oh, I'm no nurse. But a person who travels out here has to know—"

She was interrupted by a startling burst of chatter from inside my parka. I winced.

"What's that?" Laurie gasped.

Well, I thought, *the cat's out of the bag—so to speak.* But I could still try. . . . "Sick squirrel," I said weakly. "I think that's what the wolves were after. I know I'm not supposed to be carrying him around. But I saw him down in the canyon where I was camped, and I heard the wolves at night, and . . . I couldn't just leave him there."

For a moment there was no sound but the breeze whispering through the aspens. I felt Danni and Laurie sizing me up, and I didn't like being on that spot because I had begun to like them.

My parka chattered again. Laurie looked at her mother and then, accusingly, back at me. "That's no squirrel."

I sighed. "You're right, Laurie. It isn't."

"Well, what is it?"

"Can you keep a secret?" I'd already decided they probably could. I hoped I was right.

"Of course," Laurie said indignantly.

"Okay. I'll show you. Maybe we'd better go into your tent."

We went, I first fetching my noisy parka from its impromptu hook. Danni dropped the storm flaps and zipped the door shut behind us. We crowded around my parka. "Okay," I said, "I'm trusting you. Let's keep our voices down. Nobody can see in, but they can hear." I unzipped the big front pocket, and Tweedlioop's head poked out, lethargically surveying his surroundings. "Tweedlioop, I'd like you to meet Danni and Laurie. Danni . . . Laurie . . . a very special friend of mine. I call him Tweedlioop."

Tweedlioop slowly crawled out. Laurie let out a little gasp. Danni just stared, her frown not quite surfacing. I suspected they were both pretty familiar with all the local wildlife. "He has *hands,*" Laurie said.

"What is that?" Danni asked. "Where'd you get it?"

"Savage Canyon," I said, "but that's not where he came from originally. He's a long way from home—and he's an orphan."

For a while they just stared. Then Danni asked quietly, "Do we get the whole story?"

"Sure. But remember: in strictest confidence." I boiled it down to the bare essentials. "I thought he was a squirrel at first, but I didn't think he acted quite right—especially when I saw a real squirrel next to him. He ate Ziploc bags —and ignored their contents. Then he started talking to me."

Laurie cocked her head, giving me what could most charitably be called a highly skeptical look. Danni said, "Talking to you?"

"Oh, not that way. Sign language. Pretty crude—but he managed to tell me he was from outside the solar system and was shipwrecked here."

So far I'd been impressed by Danni's open-mindedness, but I could see I was stretching her limits. "You're *sure* he told you that?"

"Oh, yes. Especially when he showed me the wreck. It wasn't far from my camp. A little bitty thing—but very alien, and with three bodies in it. All just as different as Tweedlioop. He's the smallest of the bunch."

Another long silence in the tent. Outside, I heard tentative thunder in a distant valley, even as a shaft of sunlight poked through our aspens and briefly cast quivering leaf shadows on the tent. My two human companions were staring at Tweedlioop and he was staring back. I couldn't tell what any of them was thinking.

Laurie said, "Why do you call him Tweedlioop?" I told her and she said, "I wonder what it means?"

I didn't try to answer. Danni said, "So now what? You've brought him out. What can you do for him?"

My mind filed bits of data about Danni that seemed tiny at the time but on later reflection would take on considerable significance. She had not questioned my story, either explicitly or in any subtler way that I could recognize. And she asked, "What can you do for him?" Not *to* him or *with* him, but *for* him.

"That's one heck of a fine question," I said. "I don't know. I want to help him; I know that much. At least to stay alive and healthy and reasonably comfortable. I'd *like* to help him get back to his folks, but I'm not sure that's possible. Not even technically."

Danni frowned. "I thought you said the others were dead."

"Only some of them, as I understand it. A little landing boat. The real starship is much bigger, and he seems to think it's still orbiting somewhere out past our planets."

Laurie was staring at Tweedlioop with the awe of a sophisticated nine-year-old. "Wow," she breathed. "You mean this little fella came here in a starship? Just like in a movie?" Very carefully, she reached out and touched him on the head.

"Don't go assuming too much, Laurie," Danni cautioned. "There's still a lot we don't know."

"The problem," I went on, "is that whatever I do, I'm going to need help. Somebody's going to have to study him medically, and if there is a ship out there it's going to take a lot of technical support to contact it. I have no delusions I can keep him secret forever. But I don't know how I should approach the authorities." I looked at Tweedlioop, who was studying Laurie's hand. "I don't want to hurt him any more than necessary in the process."

Danni nodded sympathetically. "Understatement of the week. I haven't thought much about anything like this before, but I can see a fascinating tangle of legal problems bursting into bloom. The basic one, from your point of view, is what legal rights does he have, if any. You're convinced he's intelligent and civilized, but that won't be obvious to everybody. You thought he was a squirrel. Show him to a sheriff and he might right away be labeled *ferae naturae,* and treated accordingly.

The Latin threw me for a second, but then I recognized the roots and got the idea. "But the ship—" I protested.

"Inconclusive," said Danni, "even if they bother to check it out. All the other witnesses—if they could be considered that, which is questionable—are dead. Tweedlioop *might* be a juvenile member of the spacefaring race —or he might be a domestic animal. The burden of proof is on you, and you don't have much to work with." She paused briefly, absorbed in thought. "And of course if there *is* a spacefaring race, whether or not Tweedlioop is a member of it, the whole thing becomes first and foremost a defense question. The armed forces will want to find the ship itself as fast as possible, and everybody will have a stake in deciding the wisdom of contacting it. Tweedlioop himself will be an object of suspicion. They'll have to treat him as dangerous. I can imagine armed guards while they—"

"Tweedlioop dangerous?" Laurie objected. "That's ridiculous. He's just little and cute and—"

"And that may be the most dangerous thing about him," I said. "Because there really *may* be dangerous aliens out there, and thinking they're all cute and harmless because Tweedlioop is might be the worst thing we could do. I don't like to think about that, but I have to. And it scares me. Twice."

"He's right," Danni told Laurie. "I don't feel that's the way it is, either, but we have to think about the possibility." She looked at Tweedlioop and returned to whatever catalog she'd been thumbing through in her mind. "You know, I *did* read something about this, back in law school. Guy named Puccetti; never dreamed I'd ever have any practical use for it. His basic criterion for deciding whether a being should be treated as equivalent to human was: can it take a moral attitude or make moral judgments? You might get a court to consider that—but if Tweedlioop is an immature member of his species, can the test be applied fairly?"

"*I* make moral judgments," said Laurie.

"But you're pretty mature for your age. We don't know anything about Tweedlioop's learning curves. Yessir, Bill, you've found yourself quite a problem here."

"Wait a sec," I said, reacting belatedly to something she'd said a few sentences back. "You're a lawyer?"

Danni nodded and laughed slightly. "Yes."

My mental wheels were doing a little turning of their own now. "I don't know the protocol in a case like this," I said slowly. "I've never consulted a lawyer in the outback before. But we agree that a lot of my problems are likely to be legal. Would you think me terribly presumptuous . . ." I broke off and tried again. "Could you give me some advice on what to do? Just enough to get me through the next day or so, maybe?"

"I can try," she said, "but there's not much I can tell you at this point. It's going to be a big job, I think." She pondered. "For now, I'd say just keep him out of sight while we both feel out the possibilities. I'll tell you more as we go along—if you want me to."

Did she really mean what it sounded like? And I'd thought myself lucky when I thought she was a nurse. "But . . . I'm leaving tomorrow."

"We can keep in touch."

"Like you said, this could get pretty sticky. Are you sure you want to get involved? I could say good-bye and you could forget you ever saw Tweedlioop and avoid all the headaches and heartaches he's going to bring. That might be better, for you."

"Sure," she said. "And you could have left him down in the canyon with the wolves."

"*Touché.*" There was more and more sunlight among

the shadows on the tent. There was a lot I liked in Danni's attitude, but I still wasn't sure. . . . "Where are you located? When you're not backpacking, I mean."

"Anchorage."

"Naples, Florida," I replied, forcing a grin to hide my disappointment. "Nice try."

But she said, "No problem."

"Huh?"

"No problem. I'm interested. I'm licensed there. If you want me to do it, I'll come down as soon as I can wrap up my business in progress here. I'll stay as long as necessary."

If she was on the level—and my intuition said she was —this seemed too good to be true. If there was a catch, I'd rather find out about it now. "You're just going to take my word for all this?"

"Oh, I may take a stroll down the Savage to take a look at the wreck—but not because I don't believe you. I've seen Tweedlioop, and I know what the local squirrels look like."

The skeptic in me asked, *What's in it for her?* I asked, "What will you charge?"

"Nothing." When my eyebrows shot skyward, she added, "Maybe expenses, if they get out of hand, but that's all. I'm just interested in the case. I don't take cases I'm not interested in."

"That doesn't sound like a very lawyerly attitude."

"I went into this because I didn't like a lot of the lawyerly attitudes I saw."

I mulled that over. From her, from what little I'd seen, I could almost believe it, though my psyche's bodyguard was still wary. I knew virtually nothing of her qualifications—but I liked her attitude. My hunch said she was all right—and the fewer additional people who knew about this, the better.

I looked at Laurie and thought of something else. "You said this might take quite a while. If you go to Florida . . . what will your husband say?"

Her face may have reacted, very subtly, but I wasn't sure. "Don't have one," she said. "He died in a climbing accident three years ago."

I never know what to say to something like that. "I'm sorry." Trite and meaningless, but at least sincere.

"Thanks, but no need. I miss him, but it doesn't hurt anymore. I was with him when it happened. We took risks; we knew we took them. We were both prepared to accept the consequences if things came out against us."

That touched my personal sore spot. I hadn't, when I should have. "I understand," I said awkwardly. "I lost my wife, too."

I did not elaborate. An awkward silence fell over the tent. The thunder had missed us, and the winds and aspens were quieting down. Tweedlioop, after his initial curiosity about his surroundings, had settled back into what might have been sleep. His eyes were open, but his breathing was slow, regular, and barely noticeable.

Danni crawled to the door and unzipped it, breaking the silence. "Let's walk over to the ranger station, Bill," she suggested with a reassuring smile. "I'll corroborate your story. Laurie can watch Tweedlioop while we're gone, and when we get back I'll help you set up your tent."

III

The ranger was a little skeptical about wolves acting that way with no provocation, but he apparently knew Danni and he gave us no serious trouble.

The next day, crystal-clear and cool, Danni and Laurie saw me and Tweedlioop off on the noon train to Anchorage. We traded addresses and phone numbers as we waited in the little station, a stone's throw from the campground, and they ran alongside the train, waving and shouting things I couldn't hear as it pulled out. I hoped I'd see them again, but already I was bracing myself for the possibility that I wouldn't—or even that I'd decide I shouldn't. When the world outside my coach window fell away below the Riley Creek trestle, I had the odd feeling that I was crossing a major division in my life as well as in the landscape.

As Morino and Danni and Laurie passed out of sight and into memory, I settled back in my seat, trying to concentrate on what I was likely to encounter on the other side. I was lucky: the last car on this run wasn't a dome car and it wasn't very crowded. I found a seat near the rear where I could be alone and always see the conductor coming. As far as he was concerned, Tweedlioop didn't exist, and I wanted to keep it that way.

That, I realized, was going to be my basic problem all the way home. I had some five thousand miles to go, and it was going to get harder before it got easier. This leg was relatively simple. I had checked my full-size backpack and kept my day pack and Tweedlioop with me. All I had to do was tuck him out of sight, in pocket or day pack, when people came around. Alaska is still a wild enough mixture of frontier and modern that a lot of eccentricity passes without comment, and chances were that few passengers would make much fuss even if they saw him. But I didn't want to take chances with railroad personnel; officials tend to be officious anywhere. My one real worry was that he'd start vocalizing when he shouldn't.

I'd picked up some cheese and nuts at the little store at Morino so I wouldn't have to go to the dining car. I ate those in my seat, taking Tweedlioop out and offering him whatever he liked, including wrappers. He still seemed droopy, but a couple of times he did seem to be trying to communicate. I was sorry and frustrated that I couldn't figure out what he wanted. On the other hand, the trip was long enough for me to start learning about his sanitary needs, and I was relieved that I was able to convince him that Ziploc bags had other uses than as food.

I tried to relax and watch the scenery, but not very successfully. Tweedlioop did get noisy once in a while, and every time it happened I was afraid he'd draw attention. I felt both tentative relief and heightened apprehension as we rolled through the lush green farmland of the Matanuska Valley, stunningly lit by the late afternoon sun, and recognized that Anchorage wasn't much farther. *If he can just hold out a little longer* . . . I thought fervently.

And then I thought how painful it would be if we got this far and *then* he was discovered.

But that didn't happen. Green fields and mountains gave way to a growing density of shacks, then houses, and finally the train dragged itself into the Anchorage station and came to rest with a great sigh.

With a sigh of my own I gathered Tweedlioop and my personal belongings and exited with all reasonably seemly haste. I waited impatiently for my pack to emerge from the baggage car, shouldered it (taking care not to crush Tweedlioop), and embarked on the next leg of my odyssey.

That odd mixture of frontier and modern flavor is most pronounced, at least for me, here in Anchorage. There is a scene just as you come out of the railroad station that distills it all into a single image. In front of the station stands an antique steam locomotive flanked by two totem poles—and in the background, up a grassy hill and framed by the poles, rises the sleek tower of the Anchorage Westward, every inch the essence of modern urban hotel.

Which was *not* where I was staying.

In the shadow of the Westward, on the edge of an undistinguished section of downtown, stands a dumpy little hotel whose name I can never remember. The lobby is a cubbyhole and the decor negligible, but the rooms are clean and the prices fairly reasonable—which is something a person from the Lower Forty-eight can't say about too many Alaskan establishments.

Pack on back, I set my course thither and trudged up the hill. I checked in—no trouble, though I had no reservation—turned Tweedlioop loose in our room and suggested that he behave himself, hung out my Do Not Disturb sign, and went out for a bite to eat and a few necessary errands.

There's a nice restaurant in the Westward, decorated with murals of old mining photos, where financiers in three-piece suits eat next to lumberjacks and trappers fresh from the woods and nobody seems to notice. I'd had a good salmon dinner there when I arrived, and I had another now. As I ate it I pondered my next move and reluctantly concluded that the airlines *would* consider Tweedlioop a pet and I would have to act accordingly. I could *try* to smuggle him aboard with me, as I had done on the train, but airport security would make it a lot harder. Like it or not, my best chance of avoiding detection and investigation was to carry him as a pet, sticking strictly to the rules for such and hoping nobody would look too closely at what *kind* of pet I had.

I'd never flown with a pet before, and I had no idea what was involved. After dinner, I took a stroll around Beautiful Downtown Anchorage, hoping to find out and get the red tape taken care of so we could fly out the next day.

But it was Sunday evening, and everything was closed. So I went back to my room, with a nervous glance at the No Pets sign as I passed the front desk, and checked on Tweedlioop. His condition seemed stable, as far as I could tell; at any rate, the fluctuations appeared no wilder than before. That was a relief. It didn't look likely that we were going to get much farther for at least a day.

I sat by my window until quite late, watching the city lights come on and the surrounding mountains fade to silhouettes against a sky that was not quite dark.

I got an early start in the morning, making my rounds and learning the ground rules. There were several ways I

44

could get to Miami, where I'd left my car, with not more than one plane change. No two airlines had quite the same pet regulations. When I got down to checking seat availability, there was really only one way to get home by tomorrow night, and that involved changing both planes and airlines in Chicago. Both lines agreed on no pets in the cabin, so Tweedlioop was going to have to be checked as "baggage" in an airline-approved kennel. I didn't think much of that, and I didn't care to speculate on what the crew of his starship would have to say about it. But I was stuck with it.

Furthermore, one of my airlines required advance notification—meaning I couldn't use a flight *today,* which a good cabbie could have got us to—and both required payment, in advance, at twice the normal excess baggage rate. Naturally they couldn't assess the charges until they had the weight, but they were bighearted enough to say I could take care of that when I checked in at the airport.

They were also quite emphatic about not crowding more than one animal into a kennel, and hinted darkly that airport personnel would be on the lookout for such abuses. They offered to sell me a kennel on the spot, but the ones they showed me had a little more visibility within than I cared for. So with no flight available until tomorrow, I spent the afternoon shopping around in pet stores. I finally found something a *little* harder to see into than what the airline had shown me—but not a lot.

I looked Tweedlioop over pretty carefully in the morning, knowing we'd be separated for several hours. I kept offering him the same kinds of munchies, since I hadn't the foggiest about his actual needs. He didn't look any worse than yesterday, but still nowhere near as chipper as

I thought he should. He didn't even look as good as when I'd first met him.

A little sadly, I tucked him into the kennel with some goodies. "Not my idea," I apologized. "Hardly the kind of indignity an interstellar ambassador should be subjected to, but hang on for a day or so and I'll try to make it up to you."

I secured the lid and went down to check out—with a clerk who cast a very skeptical eye at my new piece of luggage—and hailed a cab to the airport.

The check-in woman at the baggage counter was fiftyish and as stern and hatchet-faced as my sixth-grade English teacher. She turned the kennel around twice, checking all its seams and joints. She peered in through one of the openings and frowned. "Well, there's only one in there, anyway. Plenty of food and water for the trip?"

"Yes, ma'am." She hefted the kennel onto a scale, noted the reading on a form, and started punching buttons on a calculator.

And the kennel twittered.

The clerk looked up sharply, frowning. Tweedlioop twittered again. She hauled the kennel back onto the counter and took a painfully close look inside. I held my breath. "This is a *dog?*" she said.

"I didn't say it was a dog."

"What is it?"

"A squirrel." She looked skeptical and I added, "Experimental animal. I'm doing genetics research at the university in Miami. This is a new breed we've developed. I was showing it to some colleagues in Fairbanks."

"Hmph. I don't approve of that sort of thing, but it's not my business. Customer's always right, they tell me."

She cast a sidelong glance at my pack. "You need that to go to the university?"

"More comfortable than a suitcase," I said. "Besides, you think I'm going to come all the way up here and not get out and see some of the country?"

"Can't argue with that," she granted. "Well, let's get you wrapped up here." I relaxed considerably as I watched Tweedlioop's container disappear through the black rubber curtain over the conveyor, but this lady had given me quite a scare. I didn't have much experience at lying on my feet, and I was in no hurry to get more. I'd better firm up my story in case I had another encounter in Chicago.

But I didn't. My original plan called for a sizable stop-over between planes; I was going to pick Tweedlioop up, check on how he was doing, and recheck him on my continuing flight. After my experience in Anchorage, I was having second thoughts, which kept me from fully appreciating the scenery. It was magnificent—right over the jagged mountains and slinky glaciers of southeast Alaska and the Yukon—but my mind was elsewhere.

After a while clouds blanketed the ground and I did some fitful snoozing, remembering now and then to set my watch an hour ahead to compensate for one of the time zones we were crossing. Even with the cloud cover below, I could see that the sun was tracking too fast across the sky. We got stuck in a holding pattern for over an hour, and by the time we touched down at O'Hare it was dusky and my long stopover was shot. Somewhat frantically, I consulted a ticket agent, explaining that I *had* to link up with my "pet" and would rather make the flight I had reserved but would not have time to pick him up and recheck him. This agent was a good deal more sympathetic than the one in Anchorage, and he assured me he could make sure the package was transferred without my intervention. He jotted down my claim check number and I dashed off to my gate, barely making it and hoping Tweedlioop did too.

By the time we took off, the sky had cleared and become darker than any I'd seen since leaving the Lower Forty-eight. It was far more impressive than I'd anticipated, and I watched fascinated as Chicago became a glittering box of jewels on black velvet, and then the jewels became few and far between. By the time we reached Miami, I was numb. With those boarding tunnels, I could hardly tell I was in a different climate: modern airports everywhere look and feel pretty much alike. I waited anxiously by the baggage carousel, relaxing a *little* when my backpack came off and a good deal more when Tweedlioop's kennel emerged—the last thing off the chute—and I looked inside and saw hints of motion. "Tweedlioop?" I whispered.

A faint warble came from within. And I dared to hope we were both still in the game.

Outside, I could finally tell we were home. The warm, muggy air of South Florida felt nothing like where I'd been.

It was after midnight here, but my body still thought it was only seven. I was tired and my nerves frazzled, but I was not even remotely sleepy. I would drive home right away—if my car would start after its long spell of dormancy.

It did, grudgingly. As I warmed up the engine, I debated whether I should keep Tweedlioop hidden a little longer. I decided enough was enough; I'd take my chances with the lot attendant, and if I behaved myself I shouldn't see anybody else. I opened the lid and took Tweedlioop out, cradling him in my hands and making reassuring noises. "Just stay on the seat and keep quiet," I said. "But move around. Breathe. Relax. We'll be home in a couple of hours."

I set him gently down between me and the kennel. Then I took the wheel in hand and eased us forward with a satisfying purr of engine—and some feel of having at least a little of his fate back in hands I could trust: mine. The parking attendant didn't give us a second glance, the streets were uncrowded, and soon we were humming across the Everglades on a dark, deserted Tamiami Trail. For a long time I saw nothing but straight road and that incredible blackness wrapped around my headlight beams. Occasionally I got a reminder that the blackness was really swamp, when a coon or an armadillo or an alligator skittered across the road in front of me.

And then there were the lights of Naples—but little traffic, because of the hour. I breezed through the garishness of fast-food row and then turned off into the softer light of the quiet residential areas near the beach. I threaded my way through a small maze of palm-lined streets to Otten Drive, and with a feeling of deep relief pulled into the driveway of the house I'd been renting since the demise of Kit's Castle.

I parked in the garage, shut off the engine, and went around the house checking on everything. Nothing seemed amiss, beyond the slight musty odor all houses acquire when they're locked up and empty for a couple of weeks. Satisfied, I brought Tweedlioop in, fitted him out with a padded box to sleep in, and called the police to tell them I was back.

Then, in a rush, it all caught up with me, and I realized I was both very tired and very sleepy. I double-checked doors and lights and fell into bed.

I think I was out before the last light was.

I slept until after one—which, in my own defense, still felt like eight A.M. Sunlight was streaming through windows, and I started thinking of all the things I ought to do today, by way of getting settled back in and my life back on its track.

Except, I reminded myself, I'd crossed that metaphorical trestle back by Morino, and I still didn't know much about the tracks on this side.

I started by checking on Tweedlioóp, even before getting dressed or eating breakfast. My hope was to wait until Danni got here before revealing his presence to anyone else, but I couldn't be too optimistic. Back home, by the harsh light of day, Danni was already beginning to seem like a faraway, farfetched memory. She'd been vague about when she'd come, and a part of me cautioned that it would be a pleasant surprise—or perhaps an unpleasant awakening—if she showed up at all.

Meanwhile, Tweedlioop was still looking awfully draggy. It seemed to me that if the things I was doing for him had any value, he should be looking at least as perky as the first day I saw him. Instead he seemed in a slow, steady decline, and I was beginning to worry. If it continued, I'd *have* to ask for help.

But I could wait a little longer—I hoped. He'd had a night to rest; I'd give him the rest of the day and see what happened. Meanwhile, I could start feeling for information. I made sure Tweedlioop had the usual assortment of water, food, and Ziploc bags. Then I patted him lightly and went out to the car.

The drive to the plant was longer than I would have liked—longer than from Kit's Castle—but I'd found I couldn't be too picky when I was house-hunting. The new boom in space had opened up jobs faster than housing. Just a few years ago, there was virtually nothing in my line of work in this corner of Florida. But when things started buzzing again, a canny developer named Gatesborough had snatched up a big parcel of swamp and ranch land east of Fort Myers and made it an industrial park. Nothing heavy; just applied research and light manufacturing—but a lot of that, and much of it in electronics and cybernetics.

What started the boom? The historians are still puzzling over that, and they're standing too close to see the real causes. The most popular theory is that the early shuttle flights—and OPEC—whetted a few industrialists' appetites, and when they showed what they could do in space, the bandwagon started getting crowded. It was a little rocky, at first, with federal budgets slashed to the bone; but when private promoters saw things they really wanted to do, *and* realized they weren't going to be able to finance them with handouts, they found other ways. Then Wilbur Giannelli got into the White House, with lots of ideas for easing their way, and things really got rolling.

I turned in the driveway, having driven the whole way without much conscious attention. "Gatesborough Park," the big sign out front said, but most of us who worked there called it "Gator Park." We even still saw an occasional gator in the drainage ditches. I cleared Security and threaded my way back among the boxy buildings and tropical gardens to "our" boxy building, parked in my assigned stall, and went inside.

Low ceilings with fluorescent lights; green stripe down the center of every corridor to guide the mail robot on its rounds; rows and rows of identical doors decorated with highly individual pictures, clippings, and occasional warning signs. A lot like labs everywhere, I guess. I threaded my way swiftly through the corridors, then took a short-cut across the machine shop to Sam Grogan's office. I kept moving, brushing aside small talk from the guys I worked with.

"Hey, Bill, didn't expect to see you so soon."

"How was Alaska?"

"What's with the bandages? Wolves get you, after all?" Laughter.

"As a matter of fact, yes," I said, disappearing into Sam's office with no explanation. Reasonably safe behind the closed door, I tried to smooth my demeanor a bit before I asked Cindy, "Sam busy?"

Sam's secretary and miniature bodyguard looked up with surprise. "Bill! Back so soon?"

"Yep. Alaska's pretty intense. I thought I'd come back and spend a few days loafing before I come back to work. But when I was out there by myself, I got some ideas I'd like to kick around with Sam. Is he in?"

"I'll check." A brief, familiar ritual with Cindy's inter-com and Sam's deep voice, and then I was ushered into his presence and the door closed behind us.

Sam looks gruff, with his rugged build and slightly cha-otic iron-gray hair and shaggy black eyebrows, but that's just looks. I've called him fatherly before, and I'll probably do it again. He invited me to sit and was very careful to make me feel at ease before he'd let me talk "business." That meant once more through how-was-vacation-and-pleasant-surprise-to-see-you-back-so-soon—with great care on his part to avoid reference to my bandages or why I'd gone on vacation in August instead of the usual October or January.

But eventually he leaned back and said, "Well, what's on your mind? Coming back to work early?"

"Oh, no." I tried to look casual and relaxed. "I said I was taking three weeks and I'll take 'em. But you know, when you go off and relax and have time to think, all kinds of things float up to the surface of your mind. While I was camped out miles from anybody, I found myself playing with some pretty wild ideas. I don't want to say much about them until I've done some thinking about where they might lead. But I would like to bounce a few questions off you."

Sam shrugged. "Sure, why not?" He leaned back, listening.

"All hypothetical," I cautioned, "and some of it may be worthless. But I've heard rumors, and I thought maybe you could verify them or squelch them." I paused, feeling my way. "Suppose there was something way out on the fringes of the solar system that we wanted to get a close look at. How long would it take?"

"You mean the actual flight, or that plus the time to get ready?"

"I'll consider all variants, but for now let's say just the flight, with the fastest thing that's ready to go. Or close to ready."

"The fastest thing *we* have?"

"The fastest thing *anybody* has."

"Hm-m-m. Manned? Or just an instrument package?"

I hesitated a little longer than I should have. "Not manned."

"Okay. Just instruments."

"Yes. Well . . . let's keep an intermediate option open. How about an experimental animal? Small critter—a monkey, say. Maybe even a rat or a squirrel. But its reactions might be crucial. We have to be sure it survives the trip."

"Oh," said Sam. "That makes it harder. The *Voyager*s took well over a decade—"

"But we've come a long way since then. We have better propellants, the shuttle, orbital launch facilities—"

"Not *that* much better. And the shuttle's booked up for years in advance, and—"

"Don't worry about that. This is hypothetical, remember. Suppose what's out there is so important it could bump something else's priority."

"Oh." He eyed me analytically. "I don't see. . . . Look, Bill. I still can't see it taking less than five or six years."

"But how about the competition? Other industries, other governments, *anybody*. There've been some pretty persistent rumors about what some of them have. Fuels . . . ground-based laser boosters. . . ."

"Most of them," said Sam, his voice frosting slightly, "I don't know any more than you. In the few cases where I do, I can't tell you anything. But I can tell you that I know of nothing, even in the most optimistic rumors, that would let you do it any faster. An instrument package, maybe—a little. Not much. With an animal, you're limited by acceleration. And I haven't even heard rumors about significant advances there." He leaned forward with an earnest expression that reminded me of the day he'd sent me vacationing. "What's this all about, Bill? Just between you and me."

"I told you, it's hypothetical."

"Yes. You told me so often I can't believe it. What's really eating you?"

I looked at him silently for a while, disappointed on at least two levels. "You agreed," I reminded him, "to listen with the understanding that it was just wild speculation and I wasn't going to give details."

He leaned back, but his gaze was now plainly suspicious. "Okay. Whatever it is, I hope either it pans out or you get it out of your system. Frankly, I think you would have been better off getting your mind completely off your work for the duration. I hope you will for the rest of your vacation."

"I'll try," I said, rising. "Thanks for listening, Sam. I'll try to make it worth your while."

While my subconscious drove home, I played the conversation with Sam over and over. According to Sam, the rumors I thought I'd heard were a long way from available realities. If he was right, even if the most powerful agencies on Earth decided immediately to send Tweedlioop back to his ship, he'd spend what might well be most of his life riding in a cargo hold. What kind of psychological condition would he arrive in?

Maybe, I thought bitterly, I'd been right back in Alaska —*before* I changed my mind and decided to "help."

Of course, Sam wasn't my only source of information. Maybe not even the best, though surely the best I could reach so easily. I'd have to check out the others before I gave up. . . .

Meanwhile, I thought as the car's nose swung into my driveway, there were much more immediate problems.

I checked Tweedlioop as soon as I got into the house. He'd eaten a few scraps, but I could no longer kid myself that either those or the rest had helped him. He looked worse, not better, than this morning.

Could I be sure about that? He *was* alien, after all. Does a hibernating reptile, or a pupating butterfly, look healthy? Might Tweedlioop have an analogous phase as part of his normal life cycle?

Well, maybe—but it was a pretty thin straw to cling to. As a general-systems man looking at a dormant reptile, I'd say it looked like a system that was operating in a successfully balanced way in a very low-energy mode. Tweedlioop didn't. His body, despite my lack of specific familiarity, looked like a system that was *trying* to operate on a fairly high level—and failing.

I finally admitted to myself that he was losing ground and needed outside help.

Now.

Tweedlioop's body was a carbon-based biochemical system, at least somewhat similar to ours. To evaluate how well it was functioning, and what it needed to return to normal, somebody had to start learning, in detail, how it was *supposed* to function.

Not me, surely. A medical doctor? A veterinarian?

Not an easy choice. A vet is expected to be a GP to many different species, while an MD spends years and years learning about one—and then, likely as not, spends more years specializing in a single *system* of his single species of patient. How deep and thorough can a vet's knowledge of any one of his patients be?

But then, how much would *either* know about Tweedlioop? Maybe a vet would be better, if only by virtue of being less overspecialized and more familiar with comparative anatomy and physiology and the general principles underlying them.

On the other hand, seems to me a doctor is expected to regard what a patient tells him as confidential, privileged information. Is a vet under any such obligation? I doubted it. Consider an outbreak of rabies, and a dog owner who didn't want it known that his pet was afflicted. . . .

The vet, it seemed to me, would *have* to spread the word.

It all came back to what Danni had said. Did Tweedlioop have the rights of a person—or of a dog?

Unfortunately, Danni wasn't here. And Tweedlioop, even as I watched, was looking worse and worse. His body shook; his good eye was closed; he made odd, spasmodic little noises. I couldn't read the signs with any confidence, but I feared that his condition had just taken a critical turn. I started, fighting panic, and hastily ran once more through my alternatives to a decision.

What it boiled down to was pretty simple. I didn't *know* any vets. But Roger Gordon was both my personal physician—a good one, as far as I could tell—and a personal friend. I'd have to take my chances on him.

I checked the calendar by the phone as I dialed. Wednesday is golf day for a lot of doctors, but not Roger. He even had evening office hours. He was busy, of course. I left a message with urgency all over it and hoped it would get through to him.

Then I waited, opening a can and gulping down some corned-beef hash.

Roger returned my call halfway through it. I jumped up and dashed to the phone. "Hello?"

"Bill? Rog Gordon. Having a problem?"

I swallowed. "Yeah. Thanks for returning my call so fast. Roger, I know it's unusual, but could you make a house call? Tonight?"

Sometimes you can hear a frown over the phone. "What's the matter? Are you hurt? I could send an ambulance."

"No, no! I don't need an ambulance. It's not me. It's . . . a visitor. I can't tell you much over the phone. You'll see why when you get here. But it's important, Roger. Trust me. Please."

I could imagine what was passing through his head— especially since he knew all about Kit and Les and why I'd been on vacation. I could hardly blame him if he was considering how many straitjackets to bring. But finally he said, "Okay, Bill. But you'll have to wait till I finish my office appointments."

"Sure. Thanks, Roger. See you in a little while. Oh . . . and bring as many instruments as you can. I'm not sure what you'll need."

It was two and a half hours before he got there. By then I was too frazzled to run to the door. I walked, and barely managed a nod to Roger.

He required no more urging to come in. Short and chubby, but firm, with curly brown hair and a severely trimmed mustache, he always struck me on first look as gruff and slightly intimidating. But the second look always turned up the reassuring twinkle in his beady little eyes, and now was no exception. He looked me over and smiled slightly. "You look a little bedraggled, Bill. You sure you're not the patient?"

"Very sure. He's in here." Deliberately forgoing the usual small talk, I led him into the kitchen, flipped on the light, and gestured at the box where Tweedlioop was sleeping.

Roger stared, then looked up at me, his face deeply creased. "Is this a joke?"

"No joke."

"Look, Bill . . . what's going on? You know I don't normally make house calls even for humans. And I'm certainly no veterinarian."

"And that's not a dog or a cat or a squirrel. Listen, Roger . . ."

I filled him in. I never realized I could edit my own speech so tightly—but then, I'd been over it hundreds of times in my head. I had it pared down to the bone. Without a wasted word or a skipped important detail—I hoped —I told him about my meeting with Tweedlioop. I told him about Ziploc bags and pictures in the mud and a tiny starship full of tiny alien corpses. I told him about the dilemma I'd wrestled with and how the wolves had solved it for me. I did not tell him how my "rescue" made me feel, or anything about Danni or the trip home.

Roger listened all the way through while standing there holding his little black bag. He never moved a muscle; his frown never wavered. But at the end he set his bag down on the floor, hitched up his pants, and knelt down beside the box.

"Well," he said, "I guess we'd better see what we can do."

I relaxed. He was all bedside manner now, though at times I could see little glimmers of uncertainty or frustration. He never looked at me, and I did not presume to interrupt him. Talking softly, reassuringly, saying words I don't remember to Tweedlioop, he lifted the little body onto a chair and looked at it. He poked, prodded, felt around, listened with a stethoscope. . . . Tweedlioop was awake, but he just lay there watching with a half-closed eye.

Finally Roger looked up. "I hardly know where to begin. I'd say there's a metabolic problem, but what am I supposed to do about it? I have nothing to compare it to."

"I know. I'm no doctor, but I'd guess the thing to do is learn all you can about what *is* happening. Maybe some of it will look more familiar than you expect. Or maybe when we see what substances and processes are there, you'll be able to figure out how they work."

"Not much to go on," the doctor grunted. "You know how much work it takes to get a handle on any new biological process?"

"But it's all we have."

"Yeah." He stared at his patient as he might at a box of jigsaw puzzle pieces that he suspected were all from different puzzles. "I can't promise you anything, Bill. But if you understand that, I'll try."

"That's all I ask."

"I'd like to start with some x-rays," he said after a while. "I don't even know his gross anatomy."

"Do you have an x-ray machine you can use secretly?"

He sighed. "No. Okay, I'll do what I can. Maybe some blood tests. . . ." He rummaged in his bag and emerged with a handful of plastic tubes, at least one of them vaguely syringelike. "Not many," he grumbled. "I don't know how much I dare take, but at best it'll be too little, even if I get good lab people who can stretch it."

He fitted tubes together, one of them was a needle. "Don't even know where the veins are," he muttered. "But at least he does seem to have some. . . ." He felt around in Tweedlioop's fur, picked a spot, and poked. Tweedlioop jerked, yelped, and then went passive again. A liquid, too thin and orange for human blood, oozed up into the evacuated tube. I cringed, both at the amount and at the very obvious *wrongness* of its appearance.

"Wonder what the techs are going to say when they see this?" Roger mused. He laid Tweedlioop gently back in the box, stood up, and packed the sample away. "Don't worry about it," he told me. "I'll send it to a good lab. They'll get as much information as they can, and they'll be discreet. I can understand if you want to keep this quiet."

I was a little jarred at the sudden realization of what he'd been saying. "You're not doing the tests yourself?"

He chuckled. "Don't know a doctor who does. Takes special equipment and too much time. We farm it out to labs that specialize in that sort of thing." He clapped me on the shoulder. "Don't worry, Bill. These people are professionals, and they get lots of strange samples." He looked back at the one he'd just drawn and his expression sobered abruptly. "Though probably very few *this* strange. But they'll just be testing for standard ingredients of human blood, and the amounts will come out wrong. They may need more samples later—if Tweedlioop lasts

61

that long—and they may not even *have* tests for the things that really matter."

He frowned, just as he had when he first saw Tweedlioop. "I keep thinking of things, Bill. He could be carrying some alien infection—"

"I read once," I interrupted, "that humans could catch alfalfa blight more easily than an alien disease."

"Maybe." Roger finished packing in silence, and I showed him to the door. He stepped outside and turned to face me across the threshold. "I should be excited about this," he said, forcing a smile. "Shouldn't I? Imagine . . . me, Roger Gordon, the first human doctor to treat an alien patient." But he didn't look excited. He looked worried. Maybe even scared.

"Any suggestions for what I should do now?" I asked.

"Not till the tests come back. Right now, you know more about him than I do." He glanced at his watch. "Look, maybe I could sneak him in for some x-rays tonight, with everybody gone home. . . ."

I would have loved to see what they'd show. But something made me say, "Let's wait for these results first. You've already done a lot, Roger. I can't thank you enough for coming over—and for keeping this under your hat."

But by the end of the sentence, he was walking out to his car, parked under a streetlight. If he answered, I didn't hear him.

I spent the next day digging in books—in my office, the library at work, and the public library—trying to track down my "other sources" of information on anybody and everybody's space capabilities. The results were not encouraging. It increasingly seemed that Sam was right. Evidently the far-out capabilities I'd thought I remembered had filtered into my subconscious from popular science magazines. Most of them were still a long way from reality, though a few had got as far as drawing boards—including ours.

I called Roger's office several times during the day. The first couple of times he told me the lab work wasn't back yet. Later he quit returning my calls and had his receptionist tell me he'd call when the results were in.

I drove home near dinnertime in fairly bleak spirits. There was a police car parked across the street, but I didn't think anything about it until I looked in my rearview mirror as I was pulling into the garage and saw one of its occupants getting out and walking up the driveway after me.

I got out of the car, trying not to frown. The policeman, a crisp young man in a crisp blue uniform with all the trimmings, spoke first. "Mr. Nordstrom?"

"Yes."

"I have a warrant for search and seizure on these premises." He stepped forward, unfolding a paper and holding it out.

It had to be Roger, of course. I didn't bother swearing at him, though I may have scowled a bit. I'd never imagined that I *knew* he could be trusted; I'd only decided he was the best available gamble. Unfortunately, I'd lost, and there was no point in looking back.

The description of "Object of Search" was Tweedlioop, and there was Dr. Gordon's affidavit as complainant. To my untrained eye it looked reasonably legitimate—or at least legal—though I suspected it was stretching a point or two. I pointed at a line and asked the officer, "What's this about an 'illegal alien and/or illegal animal'? You can't have it both ways."

He shrugged. "So we'll drop one when we know which is right. You don't deny that the object of search is here?"

I sighed. "What good would it do?"

He motioned to his partner in the car, who crossed the street to join us, carrying a small pouch. They paused at the door to put on heavy gloves and surgical masks. Not bothering to comment, I led them right to Tweedlioop's box. "There he is," I said. "A real terror, isn't he?"

Neither of them said anything, but one gave me a dirty look as he bent to gingerly pick Tweedlioop up, holding him at arm's length. Dimly noting that my subconscious was beginning to fume, I led them back to the door. They paused long enough for the one who was carrying the Menace to Earth to tell me, "There are no charges against you, so far. But I'd suggest you not leave the area."

Then they left.

As soon as they were gone, I called Roger Gordon. "Thanks a lot," I said as soon as he answered. "I thought I could trust you. Why'd you do it, Roger?"

"I'm sorry, Bill. I really am. I thought about it for a good long time, but I finally decided I had to. The possible implications were just too frightening. An alien infection loose on the Earth—"

"I told you—"

"Yes, and maybe you were right—but maybe you weren't. I couldn't take the chance. The risk might be remote, but it was enormous. And even if that's no problem, what if he's not the only one and the others aren't so helpless? He just raises too many questions. I *had* to let the authorities know. Don't you see that?"

"Okay, okay. But couldn't you have talked to me first? If it really had to be done, it might have gone down better if I was the one to do it. You should have given me the chance."

"No," he said. "You would have talked me out of it. You would have come up with excuses to wait, and we may not have time to wait." He paused. "Did they come and get him?"

"Yes," I said bitterly. "So now what? What about the tests?"

"Perplexing," he said, audibly relieved to be back on a professional topic. "We have some numbers. They're a lot different from any normal human. But I haven't begun to figure out what they mean. And I still want some x-rays."

"Okay. Get them. I want him back on his feet, no matter what other games we play. That's top priority. You've started the case; you finish it. I'll call the police and ask them to let you do that."

I hung up without saying good-bye. I *would* call the police, both for Tweedlioop's health and to appear cooperative for the future benefit of both of us—though I would try not to give them any more real information than I had to.

And before I called them, there was another call I wanted to try right away. I found the scrap of paper on which Danni had written her phone number. I dialed first and figured out what time it was in Anchorage while I listened to the ringing. About noon? She'd probably be awake, anyway, but she might be out for lunch, or working or shopping. For all I knew, she wasn't even back in the city yet.

I let it ring a dozen times and was about to hang up when there was a sudden click and a woman's voice said, "Hello?"

I didn't realize I'd been holding my breath until it escaped all at once. "Danni O'Millian?"

"Speaking."

"Danni, this is Bill Nordstrom. Remember?"

"Bill! How could I forget? How are you? How's Tweedlioop?"

"Not good. Did you go see the wreck?"

"Yes. I'm impressed. I don't impress all that easily, Bill, but when I knelt beside that thing and thought about what it meant. . . ." Her voice seemed to falter. She broke off.

I knew how she felt. "Are you still willing to come down and help the survivor?" I asked.

"Of course."

"How soon can you come?"

"Well, I'm winding up some things I should have wrapped up by next week. . . . But you sound tense. Is it more urgent than that?"

"I'd call it an emergency," I said. "His health was sliding steadily. I called in a doctor I thought I could trust, but he got jittery and blew the whistle. Cops carted him off a few minutes ago—Tweedlioop, I mean. I thought the warrant looked a little shady, but I didn't know how to resist it."

"I'll *bet* it looked a little shady," said Danni. "What are they going to do with him?"

"Don't know, but I'll give odds it won't be what he needs. I want him back, Danni. I can take care of him better than they can." Now *my* voice faltered.

She was silent for four or five seconds. Then, "I'll be on

the next plane. I'll call you back as soon as I know what that is."

"Great! Take whatever you can get into Miami, Tampa, or Fort Myers. I'll come and meet it. Is there a way I can pay for it now?"

"Don't worry about it. I trust you. One more thing. This is pretty sudden, and Laurie and I will need a place to stay. Could you make us a hotel reservation? Nothing fancy—just a place to sleep, and a phone to wrap up some loose ends I'll be leaving."

"Glad to," I said. "You're welcome to my guest room and the phone in my study, if you want them. But I won't try to force that on you if it makes you uncomfortable. Whatever you prefer."

"The guest room will be fine," said Danni, "if you don't mind. Let me check on these planes and call you right back. See you soon."

We hung up. I found myself thinking that either Danni was an awfully vulnerable chump, or she had an awful lot of confidence in her judgment of character.

But then, I realized suddenly, I was making just as hasty judgments about her.

And feeling surprisingly comfortable with them.

IV

Danni was as good as her word. She called me back in twenty minutes with reservations confirmed. She must have been a sight to see, trying to get ready to leave in as little time as she'd given herself. I caught a fidgety nap and made sure the guest room was presentable. Somewhere around three A.M. I set groggily forth, driving across town on deserted streets and then plunging into the blackness of the Everglades. I watched the sky redden ahead of me as I neared Miami, driving into the sunrise and into the short-term garage at the airport.

I paced as I waited. I watched Danni's plane land, and then lost sight of it as it taxied to the gate and I hurried to the "Arriving Passengers" zone. A seemingly endless stream of people poured out of the tunnel and up the ramp, and all of them were strangers.

But finally I spotted two familiar faces, and I couldn't remember when I'd last been so glad to see anyone. They looked different in "city clothes," but there was no mistaking their faces, or Danni's long chestnut hair or Laurie's yellow bangs. Danni wore a trim dark green pantsuit and carried an attaché case. She looked a lot more awake than I felt. Laurie looked unabashedly sleepy.

For a crazy moment I thought Danni looked as glad to see me as I was to see her, but then I'd been under stress and hadn't had enough sleep. I welcomed her with profuse thanks for coming, which she tossed off with a light laugh. "Nothing I wouldn't do for any red-blooded alien boy," she said. "I just hope I can help."

We started through the airport maze, following Baggage Claim signs through fluorescent-lighted corridors. "It's orange," I told her, "but I appreciate the sentiment. Just do what you can, Danni. I don't expect miracles."

She started to ask questions about Tweedlioop and the things that had happened, but she didn't keep it up long. When we stopped at their baggage carousel, she took a good look at my face and her expression turned suddenly sympathetic. "But maybe we shouldn't talk about this now. You look tired. It'll keep till we've all had some sleep."

I didn't argue; I *was* tired. I carried their bags—two matching tan suitcases, neither very big—out to the car and drove around to pick them up. Laurie rode in back and fell asleep right away. Danni rode in front and looked alert all the way to Naples. The 'Glades looked nice in the early morning light, and I wondered if she'd seen them before. But neither of us talked much.

On the way into Naples I asked her if they'd like breakfast. She looked back at Laurie, still sound asleep, and said maybe we should wait. So we went straight on home. We didn't wake Laurie until we were in the garage, and I didn't show them much of the house. Their room and the nearest bathroom were all they needed for now. I made sure they were settled in, then went to my room to collapse and take up where I'd left off at 2:30.

I didn't wake up again until midafternoon. The phone served as alarm, and the well-modulated voice that greeted me when I picked it up sounded vaguely familiar. "This is Gary Montcalm," it said. "Collier County courts. I'm calling about this . . . ah . . . animal that was picked up at your house. It raises some interesting questions and I wondered if you could come down this afternoon for a little chat."

"I'll have to talk to my attorney first," I said stiffly.

"This isn't a trial," said Montcalm. "Not even a formal hearing. You haven't been charged with anything." He paused as if momentarily uncertain. "My hope is that by talking this over informally, we can avoid the necessity for any of those things."

"Nevertheless," I said, "I'd like my attorney present, and that's not possible this afternoon. She just flew in from Alaska."

"I see. Well, I guess we can make a *little* allowance, but there is a certain urgency about this. Suppose we say tomorrow morning at nine. That's the best I can do."

"Tomorrow morning at nine will be fine."

He gave me directions. I debated whether to wake Danni and decided against it. I considered calling Roger Gordon to see if he'd learned any more, and decided against that, too. I busied myself in the kitchen, putting together an unnecessarily elaborate dinner for my guests.

They finally drifted out at about three. "Something sure smells good," Laurie said, coming into the kitchen and craning her neck to see what it was.

"Supper," I said. "Hope you like it. You two all rested up?"

"Sure are," said Danni. "I hope we didn't miss anything or cause you any trouble by sleeping so late. You could have woke us up."

"No need," I said. "A magistrate called and wanted me to come in for an 'informal chat' about Tweedlioop. He wanted me this afternoon, but I got it put off till tomorrow. Told him you couldn't make it till then and I wasn't coming without you."

"Good." She chuckled. "I can see where he'd try to handle it that way. He probably doesn't know which way to jump with a thing like this. He's probably still hoping it'll go away if he can find a way to soft-pedal it. Well, we can talk about that this evening." She sat down on the stool by the telephone. "I hope you don't mind my informality. I prefer to be comfortable when I can, and I find it hard to feel formal around anybody I met backpacking. But I'll change if you like."

"Don't be silly," I said. "I'm not much for formal, either." I was wearing shorts myself. She was dressed like a Floridian, now, in lemon-yellow shorts, a flower-patterned red halter, and sandals. She didn't look very lawyerly—she probably could have passed as a student at the local high school—but she did look very nice. And I didn't expect any trouble remembering what she really was.

She watched me puttering with the food and said, "Can I help?"

"No, thanks. You're a guest. Besides, everything's under control. Just a matter of waiting an hour or two until everything's baked and simmered."

"Sounds good. But don't hesitate to ask if there's anything I can do." She changed the subject. "Maybe I could tidy up some of those loose ends I left at home. You say there's a phone I can use? I'll reimburse you."

"No, you won't, but you're certainly welcome to the phone. There's an extension in the study, if you'd like privacy and a desk."

So I showed her where the study was and she sequestered herself in there until supper was ready. Laurie and I sat in the front Florida room and read, with the glass slid back so the breeze could play through the screens. I showed her my library and she browsed voraciously. I wasn't browsing: I was struggling through everything I could think of that might bear on alien physiology or far-out space travel or the legal status of aliens, and again I found myself frustrated by the lack of anything useful. For the first time I realized consciously that my wheels had been spinning furiously almost every waking minute since I'd got back, and I still hadn't got anywhere. If I didn't slow down, I was going to wind up in as bad shape as Tweedlioop.

Laurie gave me the excuse I needed. She hadn't been talking much; I think she sensed that I was busy and she was well conditioned not to bother busy people. But I think she also sensed what I had just realized about what I was doing to my own mental health, and as I put one book aside and reached for another she asked, "Is the beach near here?"

That drove home to me just how hard I'd been driving myself and what a lousy host I'd been. I drew my hand back from the book and laughed self-consciously. "It's right out back," I said. "Would you like to see it?"

"Sure!"

I got up and led her to the back of the house. So far she and her mother had only seen rooms at the front—kitchen, guest room, study, Florida room—with views only of the front yard and street. But what I liked best about the house was that the back of it opened directly onto the beach. The back edge was on stilts, and the northwest corner was a sprawling living and dining room wrapped in glass and a narrow balcony. "There it is," I told Laurie, gesturing at sand and palm trees and waves. "A good sunset through those windows is the next best thing to a roaring fire on a hearth."

"Wow!" she exclaimed. "It's neat. I've never seen the ocean before." Her eyes caught the door that opened onto the balcony and the stairway from there down to the sand. "Can we go out and walk on it?"

"Sure thing," I promised. "This evening, right after dinner, we'll all go out for a walk."

And so we did. By that time supper needed some final attention. I took care of that and summoned Danni from the study. We ate in the dining room, overlooking the Gulf and using the good tableware that I hadn't had out since I lost Kit and Les. Danni seemed well pleased with the work she'd got done, and duly appreciative of my culinary efforts, from shrimp cocktail to Key lime pie. Afterward they both helped clean up, and then we all went out for our walk.

It was fun watching Laurie. She really did seem never to have seen a beach before. Every breaker and shell and gull and crab was a new experience that she drank in with unrestrained enthusiasm. A flight of brown pelicans skimming low over the water was a major thrill; the municipal pier was a beckoning goal for some future exploration.

Danni was a little more restrained, but not much, and she made no pretense that her ebullience was just a reflection of Laurie's. She just liked beaches, and it was too long since she'd seen one. I enjoyed watching the two of them having so much fun, and some of it even rubbed off on me.

For a strange, wistful moment, in fact, I forgot whom I was with and imagined that my companions on the beach were Kit and Les. Not that there was much physical resemblance—Kit was tall and willowy, with freckles and coal-black hair much shorter than Danni's; and Les was a pudgy, sandy-curled boy half Laurie's age. But they both had had that same playful streak, and Les had been well on his way to developing his own version of Laurie's inquisitive, venturesome nature. I remembered when we had taken him to a beach for the first time. . . .

Kit's Castle was inland, so it took a drive. We hadn't been in Florida very long, but it had been a few months and we'd been so busy first settling into an apartment and then relocating to the Castle that we still hadn't been to the beach. One Sunday morning we both woke up with the same thought: *today* was the time to introduce Les to the ocean. "And besides," Kit added, "it's high time *we* went, too." So we piled into the car and drove off to Sanibel. We didn't even think to check tide tables, but we got lucky. The water was out when we got there, and there'd been a bit of a blow the night before, so there were lots of shells for Les to pick up. He looked startled the first time a wave knocked him down, but he looked at us to see whether he should cry, and when we just grinned he picked himself up and plunged right back in, laughing, as if to tell the sea he couldn't be discouraged that easily.

Driving back home that night, he held onto a cockle shell he'd decided fit his ear perfectly: he could hang it there and it would stay by itself. It was past his bedtime and he'd had a long day, so we assumed he was asleep until he remarked, very seriously, "I can still hear the ocean." Not very original, for an adult—but not bad for a four-year-old who'd never been told that particular fable.

What would he have been like if he'd lived to Laurie's age? A question perhaps better not asked, since it was so futile. But I couldn't help wondering, and as I did so it occurred to me that I hadn't been thinking about Kit and Les and past tragedy nearly so much since I brought Tweedlioop out of the wilderness—and when I did, the memories weren't quite so painful now. I knew what part of the reason was, but I suspected Danni and Laurie had something to do with it, too. And for that I was grateful.

For a while our conversation steered clear of business and weighty matters. But eventually the sun was a red ball perched on the horizon, and we were walking slowly along the beach, salt smell in our nostrils and wet sand between our toes, watching the last light dance on the wave tops. I noticed the way it gleamed on Danni's long, smooth hair, and revised my description of its color. Chestnut, I'd thought earlier, but now it reminded me of nothing so much as spun copper, and I thought idly that if I were a photographer I could do wonderfully artistic things with it in this light.

It was then that she said, "Do you think we should talk about Tweedlioop now?"

I did. I was reluctant to break the soothing surf-spell,

but I knew it had to be done. I told her about Roger, and the police who had taken Tweedlioop away, and this morning's call from Justice Montcalm. When I finished she said, "Well, I guess we'll just have to see what Montcalm has to say in the morning. Then we'll play it by ear." She paused. "You realize, of course, it's not at all clear how much good I'll be able to do. I may not even be able to function much as a lawyer."

I frowned slightly. "What do you mean?"

"Well, to act as a lawyer, I have to have legal proceedings to act within. That presupposes an applicable body of law—but a body of law evolves from a set of similar cases, and we haven't had many. I said earlier that I think Montcalm hopes it will go away—he's hoping he can convince himself that Tweedlioop doesn't represent an alien menace. But he doesn't really believe it, and he's itchy. If there *is* an alien threat, the longer he sits on it before he notifies higher-ups, the more trouble he's going to be in. So he'll do *something* tomorrow. If he decides there is a likelihood of an invasion, this whole thing's going to be jerked way out of our hands. I can see fancy footwork with presidential emergency powers and such, and once you get into that league, the top bananas can do pretty much what they want. There's not much that ordinary peons like me can do then—anyway by routine legal means."

I tried to imagine how President Giannelli would react to all this, and couldn't. "Then you think it may be a lost cause?"

"It *could* be, but let's not be too quick to assume it. We will have to find out whether there's a danger, of course; we both know that. But meanwhile we can try to see that Tweedlioop, as an individual, is treated decently. And there are always non-routine methods—extralegal, even, if it comes to that."

"Such as?"

"Such as publicity. Something I'd rather not resort to, but I might if I think it'll help and nothing else will."

"So you're keeping that as your ace in the hole?"

"I'm not sure it's an ace," she said, "but it's a card. And we'll play it if we must."

It didn't occur to me until we were driving into town the next morning that our "informal chat" had been scheduled for *Saturday*. Evidently Danni was right. Gary Montcalm must really be nervous.

We parked in a city lot and walked half a block to his chambers—alone, having left Laurie back at the house. His outer office opened right onto the sidewalk and had no visible doorbell. But we had hardly let ourselves into the little waiting room when a young man with a disarming smile poked his head out and invited us into the inner sanctum.

It was Montcalm. I recognized him from television and campaign posters; he was one of the few people I've met who looked younger in person. His round face and sleek brown hair were just *too* boyish; his disarming smile, I suspected, he'd cultivated as exactly that.

I introduced Danni (back in her highly civilized pantsuit) as Danette O'Millian, my attorney and legal advisor. Briskly, cheerfully, efficiently, Montcalm introduced the others who were seated around the modern stainless-and-glass table. Roger Gordon I knew. The one in the Air Force blues decorated with birds was Colonel Munro Gershaw, from some nearby base whose name didn't register.

Conspicuously absent was Tweedlioop. That was no surprise, but somehow I'd expected more official types.

Montcalm settled back in his chair at the head of the table. For a guy who'd sounded vaguely perplexed and put upon on the phone, he looked singularly composed now.

"I don't think," he began, unhurriedly but without hesitation, "I need to spell out why we're here. For obvious reasons, I don't want to blow this up into a big thing until I'm reasonably sure it's warranted. At the same time, if this affair is what it seems it might be, we can't dillydally around before we do something about it. And if we have to do that, it will become *quite* a big thing.

"Quite frankly, I'm not sure I'm the right person to be conducting this preliminary probe. It's not clear *where* it belongs. But it's been dumped in my lap, and I intend to do what I can with it.

"So far, not many people know about the creature taken from Mr. Nordstrom's house. Us—"

"Tweedlioop," I said involuntarily. Danni poked me with an elbow that said, *Don't talk. Listen.*

Montcalm ignored me and continued without a break. "—here, the medical team, the officers who picked up the animal, and their superior. As far as I know, that's all. For the time being, we're going to keep it that way."

He then proceeded to do what he promised he wouldn't, describing the story as he'd heard it from Dr. Gordon, which incorporated a good deal of garbled me. "The first thing we must do," he concluded, "is to establish whether the creature in question really is . . . ah . . . extraterrestrial. If he—or it—is, the implications will become a matter of national security, with large-scale mobilization and the risk of panic. Needless to say, none of us is anxious to open that box unless we must. If we're wrong, we could look so silly that our careers would suffer." He paused pointedly. "Yet Mr. Nordstrom has felt confident enough to tell Dr. Gordon his story of the shipwreck and what he thinks the creature is. Dr. Gordon, in turn, was sufficiently disturbed by his examination of the creature to call for an investigation. In his professional opinion, there is a significant chance that the creature is in fact of extraterrestrial origin. Do you have anything to add, Mr. Nordstrom?"

I made a few minor corrections and clarifications to his third-hand version of my meeting and conversations with Tweedlioop and my discovery of the wreck and bodies. He listened, took a few notes, and nodded. "I see. Well, I think it's clear that we'll have to look into this further. The next step we need is an independent corroboration of that part of your story that can be checked."

"I can provide that," said Danni. "I've seen it too."

"Nevertheless," Montcalm said imperturbably, "you'll understand that I need an independent confirmation from a reliable authority of my own choosing. Far be it from me to deny that you saw *something,* but there's still room for doubt about *what.* The wreck could be an elaborate hoax. The creature could be a product of advanced genetic experimentation, although"—he smiled benignly at Roger— "the good doctor considers that unlikely. In any case, Colonel Gershaw will provide the check we need. He has arranged—very discreetly—for certain of his fellow officers in Alaska to go in for an expert look at the alleged wreckage. You can provide us with a fairly detailed description of the location, can't you, Mr. Nordstrom?"

I could, but I looked at Danni to see whether I should. She nodded. "Go ahead."

I nodded in turn at Montcalm. "Yes, I can do that."

"Good. The Savage, I believe it was." I wondered with some annoyance how he knew that, but it didn't take long to think of ways. "I'll show you a map before you leave and you can mark the spot. We've already asked the Park Service to close that part of the park to everyone, including their own personnel." He smiled a bit self-consciously. "We didn't like doing that: it makes too many people curious. But it won't take long and when it's over we can put their minds at ease. Colonel Gershaw's associates are waiting for word from us. As soon as they get it, they'll go right in, do what they must, and come back out with a report. Then we can plan our next move—if any is called for."

I couldn't believe it would be as fast and smooth as that —or that what I knew they would find would help solve my immediate problem. "That's all very nice," I said, "but what happens to Tweedlioop in the meantime? At the rate he's going, the whole problem may just die out from under our—"

"If this is what it may be," Montcalm interrupted, "the death of your little friend would not solve anybody's problems. It would merely eliminate one source of information we will need. That fact should be enough to assure you that we are doing everything in our power to keep him alive and restore his health."

Repressing the urge to comment on his motives, I said, "But are you accomplishing any—"

Danni nudged me. "Let me handle this, Bill." She addressed Montcalm. "I think you'll understand, Your Honor, my client's interest in the health of the being he called Tweedlioop. It was he who found Tweedlioop, recognized him as an intelligent being, saved him from death in the wilderness, and carried him out to safety and civilization."

"And failed to report him to the proper authorities."

"By your own admission," said Danni, "there is some uncertainty about who the proper authorities are. To a person untrained in law, the uncertainties are quite reasonably still greater. To the best of my client's knowledge, having a doctor examine Tweedlioop was a perfectly logical first step. It addressed the immediate problem of preserving Tweedlioop's life, while at the same time providing a second opinion on whether a report to legal authorities was called for. Your Honor, would *you* come into this office with a report of an alien shipwreck survivor if you weren't quite sure of it?"

"Your point is well taken," Montcalm said stiffly.

"Good," said Danni, smiling sweetly. "That granted, I think you'll also recognize that Mr. Nordstrom's first concern, for Tweedlioop's health and welfare, could hardly cease upon Tweedlioop's removal from his care. If anything, it would intensify. So we would greatly appreciate any information on Tweedlioop's present whereabouts and condition."

Montcalm sighed. "Tweedlioop," he said with an expression that might have been distaste or embarrassment, "is in a very safe, secure place."

"At Colonel Gershaw's base?"

"I'm not at liberty to tell you that."

"Aha. But safe and secure, you say. Could I interpret that as 'under heavy guard'?"

Montcalm glanced at Gershaw. The Colonel said, "Of course. Why beat around the bush? If he is an alien and there are more of them out there, the military danger is clear. We could hardly do anything else, and there's no point in denying it."

"I see," Danni said blandly. "And his health?"

A long silence—too long. Montcalm, Gershaw, and Roger Gordon looked at one another, each waiting for someone else to answer. Finally Roger said, with something like the gentleness I used to associate with him, "Not good, I'm afraid, Bill. We've been doing what we could, but I'm not sure anything's helped. We don't know how to interpret his vital signs, but my subjective judgment is that he's in a steady decline and pretty far down. He shows virtually no spontaneous activity, and very little response to external stimuli. We have a whole team studying him now, but progress is slow. We're trying to learn a whole new biology in a few days, and I'm not sure whether what we know about our own is more help or hindrance."

I found strange emotions welling up in me, and no words to help them escape. I was only dimly aware of Danni saying, "We appreciate your efforts, but I don't think we can afford to continue them. I would like to request Tweedlioop's release back into Mr. Nordstrom's custody."

Just like that. Consternation broke out among our official hosts, and when it failed to focus itself, Danni seized the floor and kept it. "Gentlemen, let me elaborate. There remains doubt, you will recall, about what Tweedlioop is. Mr. Nordstrom told me about the wording of that warrant. Illegal animal or illegal alien? You're going to have to call him one or the other, and whichever you pick, I can answer. If he's a pet, he hasn't created a nuisance and he probably isn't covered by a license law. If he is, we'll buy him a license. In either case, he doesn't need to be locked up. If he's an alien, getting him off the planet would probably make you more comfortable, and it's just what *he* wants. Call it deporting an illegal alien, if you like, but *do* it. It'll make everybody happy."

"Except," said Montcalm, "that we don't know *how* to do it."

"So we get Tweedlioop back on his feet and find out. If he suggests calling his folks for help, we find out how and do that."

"But if it involves a rendezvous with other aliens, it becomes a *very* different kettle of fish."

"To tackle which we need to learn all we can from Tweedlioop—as you said yourself, a few minutes ago. You don't want him to die any more than my client does—and you can't afford it. Your doctors, by their own admission, aren't helping. Nothing to be ashamed of: he's outside their specialities. But the point is that none of us can afford to keep letting him slide, and Mr. Nordstrom had better luck, for a while and for whatever reason, than anybody else. Since the doctors have failed, it's in everyone's best interest for Mr. Nordstrom to have another chance."

"Ms. O'Millian," said Montcalm, "you're ignoring the fact that the medical facilities have far better equipment—"

"Which may be totally inappropriate."

"—and there may be a danger that this 'Tweedlioop' is carrying an alien infection."

"Which has already had ample chance to get loose and hasn't done anything."

Montcalm stifled an exasperated sigh. To my surprise, Roger spoke next, clearing his throat and leaning forward almost apologetically. "If I may, Your Honor, I'd like to say that I think we *can* rule out that threat. Our team has tested everything we could find in the animal's body for possible toxic or pathogenic effects on humans. We found nothing even remotely threatening."

An awkward silence. The Colonel shot Montcalm a heavily loaded look. "Even so—" Montcalm began.

And Danni interrupted, "Of course, Your Honor, it's your right and privilege to deny my request. But what will public reaction be if word gets out that you're keeping a defenseless, cute, sick little animal under heavy armed guard and watching him die when someone else might be able to help him?"

"You won't do that," Montcalm said suddenly, looking at Danni for the first time with unconcealed anger. "I'll forbid it. If I tell you to keep quiet, you *will* keep quiet. Look, I know we can't afford to let the creature die. If I saw any real chance that Mr. Nordstrom could prevent that—"

"I think you do," said Danni, very quietly, "and you know it. Okay, you can keep me from direct communication with the public. But if you don't return Tweedlioop to the one man who has had any success with helping him, I shall be forced to request a writ of *habeas corpus* from another court. That court will then have to consider whether Tweedlioop is a legal person to whom *habeas corpus* is applicable, and that will spread the whole issue far beyond this room—which, at this point, I think you'd rather avoid."

She leaned back, looking just a little smug. I could see she'd got to Montcalm. "That's ridiculous!" he said.

"Is it?" She smiled amiably. "Maybe so. It will be interesting to hear what the other court thinks."

He glared at her a few seconds longer. Then, abruptly, his smile returned, as bland and ingratiating as hers. *"Touché,* Ms. O'Millian. Under the circumstances, perhaps it would be in the interests of all concerned to see whether Mr. Nordstrom can in fact do anything more for the subject of this discussion. Needless to say—"

"Your Honor," Colonel Gershaw spluttered, "surely you don't intend to let yourself be swayed by this nonsense about a defenseless, cute little animal—"

"No, Colonel," Montcalm said wearily, "I do not. But I must make a reasonable allowance for the possible adverse effects of premature publicity, and I must make every effort to keep the animal alive in case we need to get information from him. The point is well taken that he seemed to do better while in Mr. Nordstrom's care than he has in ours. The reasons may be as much psychological as physical. Whatever they are, we need to find out whether returning him has any beneficial effects. Needless to say, our medical and veterinary team will continue to study the data they've collected—which I suspect will keep them quite busy, even if they're not collecting any more for a while—and Mr. Nordstrom's efforts will be carried out under strict security." He looked at me. "The animal will be brought to your house today. You will keep him strictly and absolutely out of sight of visitors or passersby, and you will make no mention of him, however indirect, to anyone whatsoever. You will admit me or my designated representatives to check on your progress at any time, and you will allow the med-vet team free access to the animal to make any additional tests or observations they may deem necessary. This entire arrangement may be revoked and the animal taken back into our custody at any time, with no advance notice, for any reason I deem sufficient. Is all that understood?"

I nodded, still so busy trying to sort out all the restrictions that it took me awhile to realize that we had won even a minor victory. "Yes, sir."

He turned to Danni. "And you, Ms. O'Millian, will be held strictly responsible for seeing that all these conditions are met. Is *that* understood?"

She nodded, this time without the smile. "Yes, Your Honor. Thank you."

And so it was done.

V

THAT, OF COURSE, CHANGED OUR WHOLE STRATEGY.
Given that Montcalm would keep his promise and we
would be reunited with Tweedlioop, our main problems
were now (1) to restore his health, and (2) to arrange some
means of reuniting him with his parent ship and sending
him on his way.

There was nothing we could do about (2) right away.
Officialdom was not about to put any effort into contacting
a group of aliens until they were convinced the aliens
existed. Even then there was a large question of what *kind*
of contact they would seek—if any.

In a way, I was just as glad not to have to think very
hard about that one yet. But problem 1, now that it had
been returned to us with all Montcalm's strings attached,
seemed suddenly overwhelming.

I told Danni so as we drove home. "So he's going to let
me try again. What if I can't do anything? What real hope
do I have? The plastic bags seemed to help, for a while,
but on the whole he's been going downhill ever since I met
him. Why should I think I know any more than the doctors?"

"Maybe you don't," she said. "But you don't seem likely to know less. Look—as you say, the bags seemed to help for a while. Maybe they just weren't enough. Maybe he needs something else that he's not getting from the local food. Maybe something he's getting is bad for him. Maybe some of it *is* psychological. Isn't it true that he seemed more chipper when he saw you as a possible source of help than after you led him to believe you couldn't do anything?"

"Well, yes, I guess it is. But—"

"Well, give yourself some credit. We don't know which factors are the important ones, but we do know he's been slipping faster since they took him away."

I turned onto Otten Drive, idly watching the palm fronds waving in the breeze off the Gulf. "Maybe," I said. "Actually, I think maybe the slide started with the trip home. . . ."

"Is that surprising? Travel's tiring, even under good conditions. Try to imagine making that trip in a pet carrier in the luggage compartment, at the mercy of alien giants and machines who pass you around and never tell you where you're going or what they're planning to do. For that matter, the shock of losing his family or crew or whatever they were, and being stranded on an alien planet, could just be catching up with him." She considered. "What we need to do, somehow, is give him back hope, either to get back where he belongs or to build a life here. That may be at least as important as medical treatment."

We pulled into the garage in silence. Looking back, I saw that I hadn't been making much effort to communicate with Tweedlioop since we'd left Alaska. But then, I hadn't really had much chance. . . .

Or was I just rationalizing again?

Laurie was waiting on the balcony overlooking the beach. She was overjoyed to hear that Tweedlioop was coming home. I wished I could be as optimistic about it as she was.

He came about three-thirty, and his escort was not what I'd expected. I didn't see the car pull up, but when I opened the door, Roger Gordon was grinning sheepishly, not quite at me. "Hi, Bill," he said. "Still speaking to me?"

I thought it over a few seconds and then laughed. He was carrying Tweedlioop, wrapped in a towel. "Sure, Roger. Come on in."

Danni and Laurie had been watching us from across the room. When I let Roger in and closed the door, Danni came toward us. Laurie started to follow, then disappeared abruptly. She reappeared carrying Tweedlioop's box, which I'd left in the kitchen. Roger laid his bundle gently down in the box and unwrapped it.

Tweedlioop lay there, breathing almost imperceptibly. He was watching us, but made no move either toward or away. I could almost imagine I saw distrust in his eyes—or at least the good one—but I couldn't really be sure.

For a while none of us said anything. With the pressure finally eased, at least temporarily, I found myself looking at Tweedlioop in a way I don't think I had before. *Who are you, little fellow?* I asked silently. *What were you doing way out here? What will you do if you ever get home?* I realized distantly that those questions were big and important, but I couldn't pursue them. For now I could only finish, *What can I do to help?*

As if reading my mind, Roger asked, "What have you tried so far, Bill? We had a whole team of fine physicians and vets working on him, but I'm afraid we didn't do much for him. The tests were a drain on him and just a starting point for us. It'll take us weeks to make any sense of them. Did you have any better luck?"

"Well," I said, "I had even less to go on. Just guesses. I've pretty much told you what I did. He seemed to have a real craving for the Ziploc bags, and they seemed to help for a while. But then he started downhill again. He kept eating them, but it almost seemed as if they turned against him."

"Hm-m-m." Roger stroked his chin. "Have to make sure the biochemists recheck the composition of those bags and where they might fit in. First they help; then they make him sick again. . . . Hm-m-m!"

"You know what it sounds like to me?" Laurie said suddenly.

We all looked at her, startled. She went right on without waiting for an answer. "It sounds to me like a kid OD'ing on candy and not getting any spinach."

I stared. It did make a perverse sort of sense—the kind that seems painfully obvious once it's suggested. But he was *alien*. Surely such a simple-minded analogy couldn't mean much. . . .

But Roger, whose first response had been a shrug, was now nodding and stroking his chin more vigorously. "Could be," he said slowly. "It's as good a guess as *I* can make at this point. Tell you what, Bill. Why don't you try this for a while? Give him as big a selection of things as you can—everything *except* Ziploc bags—and let him choose what he wants. Humans and other earthly animals sometimes develop a craving for foods containing nutrients they lack—"

"And sometimes things that aren't good for them," I said. "Like candy. Maybe Laurie's right."

"She may be very right," said Roger, "and so may you. He *is* a kid, near as we can tell—though we don't know how 'old'—and kids don't always know when to stop with the candy and ice cream. But they stop when they get sick enough. Under the circumstances, I don't see much choice but to risk it."

I didn't either, but I kept thinking of risks. "Everything we offer him will be unfamiliar. He won't know what's safe and what isn't, any more than we will. We may offer him vitamin-enriched fruit juice, and something in it may turn out to be his version of arsenic."

"Or vice versa," Roger said. "Don't forget the rat poison when you lay out his smorgasbord. And turpentine, and lighter fluid. *Everything.* Lots of choices. And take lots of notes on what he takes and what he doesn't, and any changes in his appearance or behavior afterward. Keep me posted. Call as often as you need to, anytime."

That sounded more like the Dr. Gordon I'd called in the first place. But when I thought about what he was suggesting . . .

I thought about razor blades and rat poison in Halloween handouts and shuddered. I wanted to *save* Tweedlioop's life, not . . .

Again Roger seemed to read my mind. "I know it's drastic, Bill. Don't think I'd suggest it lightly. There's a good chance it'll either kill him or cure him, and I wouldn't give you odds either way. But I don't think we have time for anything more cautious."

And so we did it that way: the Laurie-Roger untested treatment for unidentified ailment of unidentified patient.

Roger had to leave, but the rest of us laid out a banquet of every meat and fruit and vegetable and medicine and household cleaner and solvent we could think of. We set up a box where Tweedlioop could seek darkness, and a sunlamp where he could bask.

And then, with considerable trepidation, we turned him loose in the midst of it all—and sat back to watch.

For several minutes he lay on the floor, looking around and occasionally "sniffing." Finally he dragged himself across the floor and nibbled on some broccoli buds. Then he moved on, sampling, never trying much—a lick of toothpaste here, a dab of chopped liver there. . . .

I cringed when he took a sip of carbon tet, but forcefully reminded myself that it might be better for him than the broccoli or liver. And he did seem to be trying things cautiously. He was not a baby, after all; my rough guess placed him closer to Laurie's effective age. And he might well have had some survival training before he was brought here. . . .

It was all over in a few minutes. Whether it was caution toward the chemicals, or uneasiness because we were watching him, he didn't stay very long at any one sample. After trying a few, he crawled partway under a couch and lay down. A translucent film covered his good eye. . . .

I must have looked alarmed, because I moved quickly toward him and Laurie shooed me away with one hand while her other put finger to lip in silent, "Sh-h-h!" "I think he's sleeping," she said.

I hesitated momentarily, then made myself relax. She was probably right. "Maybe we should leave him alone," I whispered. "Why don't we all go out to the beach for a while?"

"Not me," said Laurie. "Somebody should watch him all the time. I'll do it now." She took a long look at Danni and me and added, "But I think you two should go to the beach. You look like you need it."

We laughed, but her prescription was again right on target. We drove out first to visit the Colonel (the *other* Colonel) and bring back some fried chicken for an early dinner. Laurie stayed with Tweedlioop to eat hers; Danni and I took ours out on the balcony. It tasted mighty good, and my appetite was in surprisingly good form.

"Worried?" Danni asked.

"Sure," I said, munching on a thigh. "But you know something, Danni? It's not bothering me like things were before. If I think about what can happen, it's scary—but I don't know a thing we can do about it that we haven't already done. So I'm just going to wait and see, and in the meantime I'm going to start enjoying life again."

She grinned. "Good."

We didn't talk much more while we finished off the chicken, but I enjoyed the chance to sit alone with her without frantically plotting our next piece of strategy.

After we finished eating, we went for another walk. We left our shoes on the balcony and started off toward the pier, sometimes walking in soft warm sand and sometimes in foam that tickled our toes. "I don't think we have to be in any hurry," I remarked. "The patient's in good hands. That's quite a daughter you have there, Danni."

She beamed proudly. "Yes, she is, isn't she?" Then, after a pause as if unsure whether she should ask: "Did you have any, Bill?"

"A son," I said with a sigh—and then, to my own

surprise, I discovered I felt like talking about it now. "His name was Les and he was four the night I lost him and Kit. They were pretty special, too. . . ."

I told her the whole story of the fire and how I might have been able to save them and the guilty doubts that had haunted me since. I don't think I would have been able to get through it out loud before, but I did now, and I was glad.

At the end of it Danni said, "I'm sorry," much as I had once said the same to her. "Sorry it happened and sorry I brought it up. It must be painful for you to talk about."

"That's all right. I needed to work it out of my system. That's why I was in Alaska. I think it worked. Tweedlioop helped. So did you. And Laurie."

We climbed onto the wooden pier and walked a thousand feet out to sea, past fishermen seeking snook and brash brown pelicans seeking handouts. I changed the subject, but not too much. "Have you always lived in Alaska?"

"Hardly," said Danni. "Would you believe I grew up in the wilds of New York City?"

"If you say so—but it's certainly not obvious. How did you wind up in Alaska?"

"Always had a taste for things like that," she said. "Actually, my part of New York wasn't all that wild, in any sense. It was a pretty nice residential area on the Upper East Side of Manhattan. But I always felt boxed in, as far back as I could remember, and it seemed to me that living all jammed together like that wasn't good for people —not for me, anyway. I knew things didn't *have* to be like that, because books and television and movies showed me places that weren't—places with private houses and grass and trees, from Iowa farms to the tundra and taiga in Alaska. One day it dawned on me that those places really existed and I had only myself to blame if I'd rather be in one of them and I wasn't. Central Park was barely enough to whet my appetite; I started plotting to get a lot farther out someday. When I was about fifteen, I found out there was some *real* country thirty or forty miles up the Hudson. After that I saved up for some hiking boots, and practically every weekend I'd hop a bus or a train up the river and traipse off into the wilds."

I didn't know that part of the country, but her description surprised me. "You're stretching the definition of 'wilds' just a bit, aren't you? I thought New York's suburbs went on forever and there was nothing very wild anywhere near."

We had stopped on the end of the pier and were leaning on the rail, watching wavelets dance and sparkle below us as the sun descended toward the horizon. "Everybody thinks that." Danni grinned. "Even New Yorkers, and that makes it all the better for people like you and me. Bill, you've got to go up and see what it's really like sometime. You wouldn't believe all the open woods there are. My favorite area's called the Hudson Highlands, where the river squeezes between rugged hills with names like Storm King and Breakneck Ridge. Only thirteen or fourteen hundred feet high, but the river's at sea level, so they're impressive. There's one state park that's bigger than some national parks. And hundreds of miles of really fine trails, where you're as likely to see deer as people—" She broke off with an apologetic smile. "Am I getting carried away?"

"Yes." I smiled back. "But I don't blame you. Remind me to ask you how to find those places sometime."

We headed back to land and made a side trip downtown so Danni could buy a few more locally appropriate clothes for herself and Laurie. We returned to the beach to finish our trip home. The tide was on its way out and we picked up a few shells for Laurie. We sat down on a piece of driftwood to watch the crucial moments of sunset, and when we got up I offered my hand to help her (as if she needed it).

The sun's last etchings paled away and the sky overhead turned deeper and deeper blue. It was quite dark and fairly starry when we got back to the house; a gibbous moon was already up in the east, but from the beach it was still largely hidden by trees.

Laurie was stretched out on the living room floor when we walked in, slowly stroking an apparently sleeping Tweedlioop curled into a ball next to her. She looked pretty sleepy herself. She put a finger to her lips and stalked over to meet us. "Hi," she said. "Have a nice walk?"

"Sure did," we both told her, and I added, "How's Tweedlioop?"

"Okay, I think. He woke up once and ate some more. I wrote it all down. Then he went back to sleep."

I felt an enormous relief, still tempered by caution, that at least things seemed no worse.

"Oh, yes," Laurie added suddenly, as if just remembering. "There was a phone call from Judge Montcalm. He said it was urgent and asked you to call him as soon as you got back."

So much for relief. I looked at Danni. She said, "Shall I call?"

I didn't argue. She did it right away, and I listened with

that nervousness typical of important conversations heard from only one side.

"This is Danette O'Millian. . . . Yes, yes, I didn't think I should put it off. . . . Uh-huh. I knew they would. Well, now what? . . , What sort of —, . . I see. Yes, I understand. . . No, sir. He won't. . . . Well, it's too early for us to say, too. . . . Oh, yes, we'll try to cooperate—but we're just as interested in what happens to him as to us. . . . Keep us posted; we'll do the same. 'Bye."

She hung up and turned to me. "The Air Force scouts went in by chopper and found the wreckage and bodies. It's official now—Tweedlioop is an alien. What that means remains to be seen. 'Wheels are in motion,' as Gary Montcalm puts it, but he won't say what they're doing or when they'll tell us more. But we're supposed to keep ourselves available."

VI

WE FINALLY CONVINCED LAURIE—MORE OR LESS—that it was neither practical, necessary, nor particularly useful for one of us to watch Tweedlioop all the time. I don't think she really believed it, but she relented when we pointed out that he might like some privacy once in a while. And so we all got some sleep that night.

We slept, in fact, until almost eleven—or at least I did. I was awakened then by a pounding on my door and the urgent calls of both Danni and Laurie. My first thought was that something must be wrong with Tweedlioop, and I sprang out of bed and into a robe and out the door in one clumsy motion.

And for once I got a pleasant surprise. Danni and Laurie were still in robes, too, apparently having hurried out to check on the patient as soon as they woke up. He was perched on Laurie's shoulder. The film was gone from his good eye, and he was holding her hair aside with one hand and scrutinizing her ear. She was giggling.

And he *talked*—for the first time in I'd forgotten how long. He made little liquid flutings and chirpings like the ones I remembered from Alaska—fainter than then, barely audible and quite unintelligible, but at least they were a break from silence. For a moment I had the impression they were so soft because he was whispering to Laurie, but quickly rejected that as fanciful. No matter: even if he was still too sick to speak louder, his dramatic improvement was the most exhilarating thing I'd seen in quite a while.

I broke into a grin big enough for three. "I think," I said, "we're over the hump." Danni and Laurie grinned back. Maybe Tweedlioop did, too, but I couldn't tell.

When the initial excitement died down, we decided to treat ourselves to a big breakfast to celebrate. We wanted to give Tweedlioop something special, but we still knew too little about his preferences to know what to offer, so he'd just have to help himself. He was more than welcome to anything I had. For ourselves, we humans fixed fresh-squeezed orange juice, pancakes, and bacon, filling the house with wonderful smells, and I put on Rimsky-Korsakov's *Capriccio Espagnole* (appropriate mood music!) as we sat down to eat. Laurie put Tweedlioop down on the carpet and told him to help himself, but within a minute he was chirping and climbing with surprising agility up her leg.

Danni laughed. "I think he likes you, Laurie."

I'd already decided that some time ago. It wouldn't surprise me if she had more in common with him than either of us. They were, after all, both children. It made me feel a little left out; but if it was true, I could only envy her. She picked him up and held him in front of her face. "What do you want, Tweedlioop? Pancakes and sausage?" She looked at her mother. "Maybe he does. Can I put him on the table?"

"I think you'll have to ask Bill," said Danni, and Laurie looked expectantly at me.

"Sure," I said. "It's his party."

So she set him on the table next to her plate and he dove right in—literally. In thirty seconds he was a sticky mess, a blob of fur matted with maple syrup and honey, and he ate so many pancakes I again began to fear for his health. The bacon he sampled, spat out, and judiciously avoided forever after; however, he did eat Laurie's napkin. I got her a new one, plus a new plate of goodies, and the four of us finished the meal in good spirits. Afterward we threw most of the dishes into the dishwasher, but I did the bacon skillet by hand. Tweedlioop took a dip in the dish water, too, which was probably just as well: he needed a bath. (I think he drank some, too.) He wouldn't let Danni or me towel him off, but Laurie managed to talk him into it.

And then we dispersed to various parts of the house to do our own things. Danni holed up in the study to do some more catching up on her Alaskan clients' legal affairs. Laurie and Tweedlioop stretched out on the living room rug and seemed to be variously playing and trying to converse. Watching them, I had the uncanny feeling they were communicating a good deal more than I had—and I wondered idly where it might lead. I also recognized that Tweedlioop was still not quite up to par. His voice was weak, he seemed to tire easily, and sometimes he seemed more to drag himself from one place to another than to walk. He hadn't beat the reaper yet, I warned myself, and there was still plenty of danger in letting him try new things. The future still had lots of room for shocks—but the present was a quantum jump above the past.

I decided I should tell Roger, so I rang him up and

described my perceptions of Tweedlioop before and after. "Hm-m-m," he said. "I'm not too surprised. Relieved, though, I must confess. Do you have any idea what did it?"

"Not really. Laurie can give you a rundown on what he ate and what he avoided and where he's been hanging out, if you like."

"I don't think that's necessary, just now, but keep taking notes. He could have a relapse, and we'll want to run some correlations in a hurry then. As long as he's improving, let's just be thankful and keep his feeders well stocked. Whatever turned him around could be anything, or a synergistic combination of several. It could even be that he had some childhood disease and the fever finally broke. We wouldn't know a fever if we saw one, in him."

So we let things ride. As I hung up I remembered we were expecting another call from Montcalm at some indeterminate but probably not distant time. That made me reflect on how far and fast knowledge and concern about Tweedlioop had spread. Barely more than a week ago, I had been the only human who knew of his existence—and I could have kept it that way. How many knew now? Danni, of course; and Laurie; and the check-in lady in Anchorage; an indeterminate number of baggage handlers; Roger Gordon; at least two cops and probably more; Gary Montcalm; Colonel Gershaw; at least one additional doctor or vet . . .

And now at least a couple of Air Force people in Alaska. More than a dozen, already—plus some National Park people who at least had suspicions raised, plus who knew how many others who had talked to any of those I'd thought of. . . .

And possibly *awesome* numbers involved in the "wheels" Montcalm said had been set in motion.

Looking at Tweedlioop lying quietly on the floor with Laurie, it was hard to believe that such a little ball of fluff could create such a stir. But I'd recognized even before I brought him out that it would happen and would just have to be got through. What had happened so far was just the beginning—and I was very impatient to learn just what wheels *had* been set in motion.

But hours went by and Montcalm didn't call.

I fidgeted a good deal, in spite of myself. I remembered belatedly that there was a Sunday paper and tried to concentrate on reading it. Laurie took the color comics and spread them on the floor. Tweedlioop crawled around on them, scrutinizing. Several times he burst into twitters and hand-waving. He finally settled down when Laurie started talking quietly to him, reading aloud and pointing and explaining, and he looked for all the world as though he was trying to absorb everything she said. When I ran out of newspaper I wondered whether the phone was out of order and not taking incoming calls, so I walked out to a phone booth and called Laurie to make sure it was working.

A little while after I got back, Danni emerged from the study. "That's enough work for a Sunday," she announced. "No word from Montcalm?"

"No. Do you think we should call him?"

"Hm-m-m." She looked pensively at me, then at Tweedlioop (now asleep in the "cave" we'd made for him), then back at me. "No. I think we should all go swimming."

"Huh? What if he calls while we're out?"

"Then he can try again later. He didn't order us to sit by the phone every minute, and I don't think Tweedlioop is directly involved in any red-alert emergencies at the moment. Laurie and I've been in Florida for over two days, staying right on a nice beach, and we haven't been in the water yet. Now I ask you, doesn't that seem a little unpatriotic?"

"Well, I—"

"Of course it does. Well, I bought us each a swimsuit yesterday, and I think we should try them out. And *you* obviously need to relax, so I think you should join us."

She was right, of course. I made myself smile. "All right. I do it on my counsel's advice."

Fifteen minutes later we were all appropriately attired and headed out the back of the house, leaving everything locked and windows covered so Tweedlioop couldn't attract any attention if he woke up. Laurie broke into a run as soon as she hit the sand, and Danni and I followed, all three of us plunging into nicely vigorous surf. The water was warm and I started feeling better almost right away. Beaches are wonderful and water's even better: they *always* make me feel better. I was startled to realize that *I* hadn't been swimming since I'd got back, and before that I'd gone every afternoon, without fail. I resolved to get back to it henceforth. Rushing around frantically is pretty pointless most of the time, and even when there's a need for it, there's just as much need for the antidote.

We stayed in for an hour or so, swimming, splashing, riding waves, laughing. Laurie got an even bigger kick from the pelicans this time: a formation of six skimmed by just to her right, so close we could feel the wind from their wing beats. I told her about the virtually tame ones that hang around on the fishing pier, and promised to take her there to feed them.

It was a warm evening and we didn't bother to change out of our swimsuits. We got some more food from the Colonel and this time shared it with Tweedlioop (who was especially fond of wings and moist towelettes). We sat around quietly most of the evening, and it occurred to me that anyone looking in from outside might take us for an ordinary family with a slightly unusual pet but otherwise quietly pleasant lives.

Tweedlioop went back to sleep about nine-thirty, and Danni and Laurie an hour later. I stayed up another hour, still waiting for the phone to ring. Eventually I gave up and went to bed. Only when I was sound asleep did the call come—and then it was not the one I expected.

"This is *who?*" I said crossly. I was still groggy, and my first thought was of midnight pranksters.

But the voice repeated, just as calmly, "Wilbur Giannelli. The President. Is this William Nordstrom?"

"Uh . . . yes." I tried to wake up and pay attention. I hadn't expected things to progress that far beyond Gary Montcalm that fast. Now that they had, I wasn't sure whether to be relieved or scared.

"Good," said President Giannelli. His voice was as smooth and calm and carefully controlled in a midnight phone call as in a campaign speech. "I suppose you know what I'm calling about."

"Not exactly," I half-lied.

"I believe you have a houseguest you call 'Tweedlioop.'"

"Yes."

"I'd like to meet him—and you. I can send a plane for

you. No need for you to arrange transportation to the airport—someone will pick you up at home. How early can you be ready?"

This was all happening pretty fast, especially for someone in my condition. "You mean . . . tomorrow?"

"Yes. It's important, Bill. You know that; I can't over-emphasize it. When can you be ready?"

"Well," I said, stalling as I tried to sort things out, "I can be packed pretty early. But . . . am I going to be away more than a day?"

"Probably. There's a lot to work out, and we can only guess how long it will take."

I felt a lot wider awake now. "Then I'll have to make some arrangements to be away from the house. And my job." I was already making a list in my mind: *post office, paper, Sam.* . . . "What can I tell people? I've been back from vacation less than a week and I'm supposed to be back at work tomorrow. You don't want to tell my boss the truth, do you?"

"I think that would be premature," said the President. "Do what you can with sick days or extra vacation or something like that, and we'll help when you've stretched it as far as you can. Hopefully we won't need you very long."

But if you need Tweedlioop, I thought, *I'm staying with him.* I remembered the question I was supposed to be answering, completed a rough mental calculation, and said, "Will nine-thirty be all right?"

"Nine-thirty will be fine. Your escort will arrive in an unmarked car. He will call himself Aristotle Buzanowski and will take you to the airport and get on the proper plane with you. Do you have any questions?"

I had plenty, but I doubted that now was the time to ask them. "I won't be alone," I said. "My attorney is here with her daughter. I trust there won't be any problem with their coming along."

"No problem," said Giannelli. "Just be sure they're all ready at nine-thirty."

"And I suppose we'll have to arrange for a place to stay—"

"Don't worry about it. That's all taken care of."

"Oh." I wasn't sure I liked the sound of that. "Then I guess we'll see you tomorrow. May I ask where we'll be going? The White House? Camp David?"

"I'm afraid," said the President, "the White House and Camp David are too well known. We'll be using something a bit more secure. It's not necessary for you to know its location. Your pilot knows where he's going."

After a few more words, of little consequence, Giannelli was replaced by a dial tone. I was surprised to find that my heart was beating at a pretty good clip. I'm not the type to be dazzled by talking to a President, but Wilbur Giannelli was one of the few politicians I'd ever actually admired.

And for the first time, I had the feeling that wheels really *were* in motion.

After I hung up it occurred to me that I had no proof that I'd actually been talking to Giannelli—just the feeling that he'd sounded right. A clever enough impostor could have fooled me, and if word of Tweedlioop had somehow spilled outside the channels I knew about, it was not inconceivable that someone less than presidential might have designs on him (and me).

I managed to avoid dwelling on that unpleasant but

(I hoped) remote possibility, but I still didn't get much sleep.

I woke my human guests at seven, tapping on their door and calling their names softly until it opened. Danni stood there in her robe. "Good morning?"

"Morning," I said. "We got our call about midnight. Not Montcalm—Wilbur Giannelli."

Danni didn't bat an eye. "I thought he might. Soon, I take it. Here or there?"

"There, wherever that is. He seems awfully concerned about security. He's sending a man at nine-thirty who will get us onto a plane bound for somewhere. They're arranging lodgings. I thought you and Laurie might like some time to pack."

"Hm-m-m. A little more cloak-and-daggerish than I'd hoped for, but I guess it's to be expected. Not much we can do about it. Giannelli seems reasonably on the level. Okay, we'll be ready."

She went back in to wake Laurie. We breakfasted together, and then I went out to do my errands while they packed. Sam was the hardest. I called him at home and fed him a half-baked story about a sick aunt. I should have known he would be ever so concerned about my family's welfare, and I had to fake a lot of corroborative detail that I hadn't worked out in advance. I think he was at least a little suspicious.

Nevertheless, I got everything passably tidied away and was back home by nine. Danni and Laurie were all ready to go, and Aristotle Buzanowski was right on time. A wiry, serious-faced young man in a blue-gray business suit, he introduced himself without smiling and flashed Secret

Service credentials that really did show that name. He carried our bags out and put them in the trunk of his green Chrysler. Danni and Laurie and I all crowded into the backseat, with Tweedlioop in his kennel on our laps. There was another agent in the front seat, but he didn't say a word or look back all the way to the airport.

Our plane was waiting with open doors, a DC-3 with no more identification on it than an N followed by five digits —an unlikely choice for an important government mission, which I suspected was precisely why it was chosen. We were hustled aboard and assured that our bags would be cared for. We had a comfortable booth with facing seats near the middle of the cabin. The space fore and aft was overrun with visibly armed soldiers, which made me almost as uncomfortable as it made Laurie.

As soon as we were aboard, they hauled in the gangplank and started taxiing. No reassuring chatter from captain or stewardesses; we just took right off. I remember a pang of regret as the ground fell away that I hadn't even had a chance to take Laurie out on the pier.

We hadn't gone far when it became apparent that the plane wasn't flying like a DC-3. It was obviously souped up a bit, but it was still staying lower than most commercial flights these days—perhaps to avoid close scrutiny by air traffic control.

None of us talked much en route: I think being surrounded by soldiers inhibited us. I looked out the window, trying to figure out where we were going. I know the lay of the land pretty well, but I didn't have a map, and some places were clouded over and the pilot made a few "extra" turns, likely to confuse us as well as anybody else who might be watching. When we finally set down, I could only guess that it was somewhere in the mountains of south-western Virginia. The runway was unusually short, and trees crowded close in around it; and though it was hard-surfaced, the pavement was painted soft green. Somebody, pretty clearly, didn't want it to be obvious.

Buzanowski led us through a rhododendron thicket on a winding path carpeted with reddish wood chips. A mockingbird was playing with phrases somewhere in the trees. Eventually we came out on a narrow street with no sidewalks and an asphalt surface that had been too long without repair. A dozen or so old houses lined the street —clapboard, tar paper, a couple of brick—each with a small, imperfectly manicured lawn. In the middle of the cluster was a tiny general store with two gas pumps out front. Beyond the houses in either direction, the road disappeared around a wooded bend. Obviously the very epitome of a sleepy little backwoods hamlet—and there-fore, said my newly suspicious nature, clearly something else entirely.

"In here," said Buzanowski. We followed him up a marigold-lined walk to a porch where an old woman was knitting in a creaky rocker. "Howdy, Maude," he said, and she smiled him a silent greeting. He held the screen door open for us and we found ourselves in a faintly musty-smelling room with a pendulum clock ticking loudly on the wall.

"This way," said our host. In a kitchen full of faint old-fashioned smells, he opened the door of a shallow pantry. He grasped a jar of home-canned pickles in each hand and lifted both at once, and the whole back of the pantry slid aside with a mellow hum. Laurie gasped. We crowded into a small but sleekly modern elevator. Buzanowski touched buttons, the door slid shut, and we dropped abruptly a good many levels.

At the bottom we stepped out into a small room—quite modern—where a very ordinary-looking receptionist sat at a desk. Buzanowski nodded and told her, "The President's guests are here."

She seemed to be studying some sort of indicator on her desk before she answered. Then she nodded and pressed a button on her intercom. "Mr. Buzanowski is here, sir. With guests."

"Excellent," said Giannelli's voice, with only slight electronic distortion. "Show them in—and have lunch brought in right away."

We were ushered into The Presence. It was a very roomy, very comfortable, and (I suspected) well-armored office, thickly carpeted and elegantly appointed. American landscapes and a couple of spectacular space scenes hung on paneled walls. A couch and several upholstered chairs faced a massive desk in one corner. In another, a table was elaborately set for five. Waiters were already appearing from a door behind the table, carrying steaming silver bowls. Wilbur Giannelli rose from his chair behind the desk and came around to meet us. "Wilbur Giannelli," he said, extending a hand and smiling. "Thanks for coming."

"Bill Nordstrom," I said, taking his hand. "My attorney, Danette O'Millian, and her daughter Laurie." I was a little surprised—and somehow pleased—that Laurie looked quite at ease.

"Pleased to meet you all," Giannelli smiled. He was a little shorter and a little older than I'd expected, but still pretty youthful-looking for a President. His smooth black hair had only touches of gray at the temples. (Persistent rumors held that the color was doctored, but opinions varied as to whether the gray or the black was dye.) "Did you have a pleasant trip?"

"Interesting," I said. "Is this whole town a front?"

He grinned. "Of course. Everybody here is Secret Service or something comparable. Even Maude. Not what you expected, huh?"

"Not quite."

"That's the idea." He bent to look into the airline kennel I was carrying. "And this, I presume, is our friend from outer space?"

"Yes." I set it down and opened the lid. "Tweedlioop."

"Well, glad to meet you, Tweedlioop," Giannelli said affably. "I hope we're going to be friends." His easy manner didn't fool me: there was plenty of worry behind that statement. He straightened up. "Why don't we talk over lunch? I didn't know how to plan for Tweedlioop, but if you can make any suggestions, he's welcome to the fifth place."

"We'll have to put him on the table," I said, "if you don't mind. He doesn't know human table manners and he has some odd tastes. But that's how we've been treating him at my house."

"Good enough," said Giannelli. "Tablecloths can be washed, and a statesman has to be flexible."

We moved to the table and sat down, Giannelli at the head. Tweedlioop and I started out on one side, and Danni and Laurie on the other, but Tweedlioop quickly scampered across the linen to Laurie's place and refused to budge. Danni shrugged and moved next to me.

The staff served and we all dug in, Tweedlioop more literally than the rest. Noticing Giannelli's amusement at his antics, I thought, *His appearance is really a problem. Everybody thinks of him as a pet—even us. But he isn't, and if we don't all realize that pretty soon, we're apt to get our noses rubbed in it.*

"I think we all realize," Giannelli said as he tasted the delicately seasoned chicken casserole, "that Tweedlioop is the reason we're all here. I'm here because it's my job, and the rest of you are here because you're the best start we have on communication with Tweedlioop and his . . . uh . . . people. Does he understand English?"

"He's probably picking some up," I said. "Mostly we use improvised sign language and charades."

"*I* talk to him," said Laurie.

"That's nice," said the President. "That will be our top priority, of course. We have to find out as quickly as possible who else is out there and what they want and where we stand. Meanwhile, I gather we can talk freely. How much have you been told about what's happened?"

"Not much," I said. "You call was the first I knew that you had become involved. A day before that, Judge Montcalm told us the wreck had been confirmed. We didn't hear anything in between."

"Well, I think it's time you did. As you know, Justice Montcalm and Colonel Gershaw arranged for some Air Force contacts to go in and find the wreckage. Their names are unimportant, but one of them was the commanding officer of his unit and so was able and obliged to initiate a course of action based on firsthand information. Naturally he made immediate arrangements for a thorough study of the wreckage and the alien bodies found in it; that is in progress now. He was also obliged to notify not only Montcalm but the governor of Alaska of his findings. Montcalm was similarly obligated to notify the governor of Florida. Both governors immediately began to mobilize their state militias, without telling anyone the reason for the mobilization. They independently reported their actions to me, thereby confronting me with the decision of what to do next. I've begun by similarly mobilizing the U.S. armed forces to meet a possible unspecified threat and suggesting to governors that the militias of other states do likewise. Now I have to decide whether to alert anyone beyond our borders. I don't mind telling you I'd like to know a lot more than I do before I make that one. It would have been nice to know even earlier, because the things we've already done can't be hidden very well. But I couldn't risk waiting."

"I think you're jumping the gun," said Laurie. "I don't think Tweedlioop is a threat."

"Maybe we'd better listen before we talk," Danni suggested pointedly.

"That's all right." Giannelli smiled blandly. "I want to hear any ideas anyone has. I agree, Laurie, that Tweedlioop himself is probably not dangerous—though we can't afford to assume even that. A German orphan in one of the World Wars wasn't very dangerous, either—but his uncles and their friends were. We need to know about Tweedlioop's uncles. You three have been associated with him more than any other humans. Do you have any observations or impressions that might help?"

We were all silent for several seconds. Then I said, "If I interpreted correctly, he tried to tell me that there are —or were—others in an orbit on the outskirts of the solar system. He seemed to want help in getting back to them."

Giannelli nodded. "We've already started checking that

out. Every major observatory in the country is scanning a piece of sky whenever conditions permit. Green Bank, Arecibo, the VLA, and orbiting scopes are working around the clock. Nobody's found a thing. They're still looking. Meanwhile we need contingency plans in case they do find something."

Danni was frowning, but stayed in the background, listening quietly until she needed to speak on my—or Tweedlioop's—behalf. I said, "Suppose you find something. Will you shoot first or try to ask questions?"

"That depends," said Giannelli, "on what we find. If we perceive an immediate threat requiring immediate defense, we will act accordingly. But we'd like to consider that a last resort. We must also consider the possibility that the alien fleet, if there is one, is not a threat but a promise." He smiled thinly. "You will recall, perhaps, that I have been a rather vigorous advocate of man's expansion into space."

I nodded. "Yes, sir. That was a major reason why I voted for you."

His smile broadened a little. "I appreciate that. Anyway, it's conceivable that whoever's out there—if anybody —has no intention of harming us. Perhaps we could even gain something from them—like knowledge. A few pointers from them could save us decades, maybe even centuries, in our own efforts. To say nothing of resources we wouldn't have to waste on blind alleys."

It sounded good. Why was my subconscious balking?

"Naturally," Giannelli went on, "we can't assume that. But if it should turn out to be the case, we should be prepared to take advantage of it. Do you see the dilemma this poses, Mr. Nordstrom?"

I thought I did, but I said, "I'm not sure."

"I think I do," said Danni. "If they're a danger, you'll want to enlist the aid of other countries in a united defense of Earth as soon as possible. But if they're a potential source of knowledge, you'd like to keep as much of it as possible for us—to use what we can to our advantage, and share only what we can share without hurting ourselves."

"Exactly," said Giannelli. That was part of what was bothering me, but I sensed that there was more, too. "Two diametrically opposite courses," Giannelli was saying, "and I need to pick the appropriate one as soon as possible. But I won't know which *is* the appropriate one until I know what the aliens want and what their capabilities are. I'm hoping you and Tweedlioop can help me find out." He studied Tweedlioop, who was wallowing in his casserole and occasionally rolling about on his fine linen napkin, with a strangely despairing expression.

"Tweedlioop is just a kid," I pointed out.

"Is he? Oh, I'll grant you he's an immature member of his species. But is he *just* a kid? Would just any kid be one of four members of a species sent in to visit an alien world with intelligent natives? Or is there something special about him?"

I thought about that. I didn't know.

"If he's *not* something special," said Giannelli, "I have doubts that there's going to be any friendly contact, or maybe any contact at all. If he's nobody, they're not going to put much effort into getting him back, either in a daring rescue or a cooperative effort. But if they view him as special enough, his safe return may be worth quite a bit to them."

"Supposing we find the ship or fleet or whatever it is,"

I said, "and they are interested in getting him back. Might we be able to take him out?"

"Not practical," said Giannelli, confirming the conclusion Sam and I had already reached. "It would take too long. It would also cost too much. It would be a flashy gesture of goodwill and would really wow some sentimental types. But in the long run we could never justify it to the taxpayers unless we were getting something of demonstrably comparable value out of it. I personally think we might. I'd like to see us stretch our muscles to that extent; and if Tweedlioop's important enough to make his folks want to repay us with a *lot* of know-how, it could be well worth the effort. But I don't think it's going to come to that. If they want him back, they can come and get him a lot faster and easier than we can send him out."

"If we contact them. And the question now is how we do that."

"And whether we want to. My military advisors have serious doubts about the advisability of calling attention to ourselves before we know more."

"How are we going to learn more if we don't get in touch?"

"Quite possibly by looking and listening without talking."

"But they obviously already know we're here."

"But they may not know that we know they're here."

I sighed, beginning to feel frustrated. "What if we don't try to contact them, and they find out on their own that we're holding Tweedlioop? It would be less than obvious that we were trying to help. . . ."

"That would be awkward," Giannelli agreed. "You may be sure my advisors and I are giving plenty of consideration to questions like that. I'm sorry that those discussions must be closed, for the time being, but I'm sure you'll understand the reasons."

There was a long, fidgety silence. We all seemed to be watching Tweedlioop in his plate, looking like anything but the focus of interstellar intrigues. *What is he thinking?* I wondered. *He hasn't said a twitter through all this. Has he lost interest in getting home? Has he not figured out that we're in a center of power, and what happens here will determine a great deal of his future? Has he given up and decided to just roll with whatever punches come along?*

Or could it be that he's still as determined as ever but he's put his trust in me to do whatever I can and take no more initiative of his own until I give the sign?

I didn't want to think too hard about that.

Eventually Giannelli started talking again. "Whether or not we eventually want to contact them, we'll want to have the ability. I've arranged for a team of linguists and biologists to make an intensive study of Tweedlioop. Naturally this will require that he be taken into government custody, for his protection as well as national security and the convenience of the researchers—"

"I hope I can talk you out of that, Mr. President," said Danni. We all looked at her, surprised. She'd been so quiet I'd almost forgotten she was there.

"Yes, Ms. O'Millian?" Giannelli said coolly.

"If Tweedlioop is going to be of any use to you in any of the options you've mentioned," she said, "the paramount concern is his physical and mental well-being. In our experience so far, those have deteriorated whenever he's been separated from Mr. Nordstrom, me, and my daughter. I strongly recommend that such a separation not be attempted again."

The President frowned. "Do you have any evidence to support this request?"

"I suggest you talk to Dr. Roger Gordon in Naples."

"I may do that." Giannelli pulled a plastic box from his pocket, punched several tiny buttons, and laid the box on the table in front of him. The waiters had reappeared and were taking dishes away and bringing bowls of chocolate mousse heaped with whipped cream. "Exactly what are you suggesting?"

"Tweedlioop's condition and progress have been best during the past few days, when he was living with Mr. Nordstrom and my daughter and I have been staying in the guest room there. Tweedlioop has been in frequent contact with all three of us. We don't know which of us has had what effect on him, but we do know this combination has produced the best results yet. I suggest that you give it a chance to keep doing so by providing Tweedlioop with living arrangements as much as possible like what he's become used to."

"That may be possible," said Giannelli, pondering. "Even if Dr. Gordon recommends it, though, Tweedlioop will have to be made available for testing and study for several hours each day."

"Of course," said Danni. "My only point is that the tests and studies may be more productive if Tweedlioop is housed among friends during off-hours rather than in a lab cage. We're the only friends he has here. And we mustn't forget that he is an intelligent, sensitive being."

Giannelli nodded slowly: evidently she'd struck a sensitive spot. "True. It *is* easy to forget, isn't it?" A light was blinking on his electronic toy. He pressed more buttons, studied a display, and looked back at us. "It seems we will be trying your suggestion, Ms. O'Millian. Thank you for making it Mr Nordstrom, I'd guess that you're going to be here a bit long for conventional excuses. We'll start covering for you as soon as you think it necessary."

VII

OUR NEW QUARTERS WERE PART OF THE COMPLEX, with all that implied, but they were reasonably comfortable. We didn't feel like we were in jail unless we thought about it too long, or on the rare occasions when we wandered far enough to glimpse a high barbed-wire fence behind a rhododendron hedge. On the face of it, we had a little brick cottage with a porch, flowered wallpaper, and pale yellow Cape Cod curtains. During the day, the human members of our "family" actually used the ground-level rooms and the porch, with its old glider that constantly craved oil. But the real living quarters—where we slept and where Tweedlioop was confined when he wasn't out being studied—were underground and as impenetrable as the President's hideout. They were not, of course, that lavish. "Sterile modern" might be a better description, and Danni early and often regretted aloud that she'd had no chance to bring some of her own things to liven them up. Tweedlioop did have some special concessions, to let him keep choosing from lots of options; I suspected he was also under frequent surveillance. Each of us had a private bedroom, but none of them was as big as the ones at my place in Florida. And, of course, we didn't have the Gulf Coast in the backyard.

There was no real office, either, which we first thought was going to cramp Danni's style. It turned out not to matter, because our keepers had already decided to cramp her so much that the lack of an office was meaningless. Not surprisingly, Giannelli did invoke emergency powers. Danni was given access to facilities for a very limited time for the sole and express purpose of winding up the affairs of her Alaskan clients or putting them on indefinite hold. She didn't like that—to put it mildly.

I was there when she stormed into Giannelli's office, a five-foot flaming tornado determined to get right to the top. But the door was well barred and the secretary on that shift was a huge, immovable, annoyingly calm man. "I understand how you feel," he told her blandly, "but the President was quite clear. There's nothing more to discuss."

"But I can't just drop those people in midstream!" she protested. "They—"

"They can find other lawyers. And you needn't worry about your lost fees. The government will reimburse you for your inconvenience."

"It's not the fees," Danni stormed. "My work is important to me because my clients are important to me. I care about those people, and I have to finish what I've started with them."

The secretary's thinly veiled sneer made clear how much he believed that. Danni kept trying for a while, but that one she didn't win. And when it became clear that she had no real choice except to do as she'd been ordered, she quit complaining and did it.

And then she settled down to fighting Tweedlioop's fight, though she was no more confident than I of its successful outcome.

At first it was just more waiting. Days dragged on and things presumably happened, but we were neither invited to participate nor kept informed. There were "closed hearings," presumably concerning the matters we had discussed with Giannelli. We were not told who attended them or what transpired. We sometimes saw Giannelli, briefly; he was always amiable but tight-lipped and in a hurry.

Every day Tweedlioop was taken away, through underground passages that linked our quarters to the rest of the complex, to be studied. We never knew much about what happened to him during those several hours a day, but Danni and I several times had to try to allay Laurie's fears (though we privately suspected they weren't so far-fetched). He was always picked up and brought "home" by a pair of technicians and an armed escort. They weren't very communicative, and Tweedlioop's reactions to them varied. Sometimes he went willingly, even eagerly; sometimes with resignation or indifference. Once he seemed positively terrified and was literally carried off by force while Danni and I held Laurie back. His escort had obviously been instructed to keep quiet in our presence, but we overheard an occasional terse remark that suggested the studies were not going well. A couple of times one of the principal investigators called to ask me strange questions about my experience with Tweedlioop, and I answered him as best I could. He wouldn't say much, either, but the terms in which he couched his "no comments" suggested that he too was frustrated.

While Tweedlioop was away, the rest of us were free to roam the neighborhood, though no doubt under scrutiny and within fixed boundaries. Those boundaries happened to be far enough out and contain enough that we were not always conscious of them, but we did get occasional reminders that security was tight though unobtrusive. There were woods and streams and farms, and the general store felt like a real one even though we knew the loafers on the porch and inside were really secret agents; and with those things we filled our days.

When Tweedlioop came home in the evenings, he almost always went straight for Laurie. Again I felt a little left out, but when we made him stay close to all of us he got fidgety and once or twice noisy and destructive. So we let him spend most of his free time with Laurie. They both seemed to enjoy it, and we could see no harm in it. Often they would go into her room and close the door, and I would hear her talking quite earnestly to him, and him twittering back.

At such times Danni and I might sit in the living room upstairs, or out on the porch glider, reading the papers. Yes, we did get papers from outside; and as far as I know, they were authentic and undoctored. There was never any mention, anyway at first, of what was happening here. That was hardly surprising. You don't expect to see headlines about discussions held behind closed doors about a subject that is not supposed to exist.

On the fourth evening we started noticing little items that didn't quite fit—little ripples on the placid surface. Not headlines—just little items like various governments claiming that their spy satellites had noticed unusual U.S. military activity and making guesses and accusations about what it meant. Danni and I remembered what Giannelli had said about mobilization at many levels, and we didn't like the implications. By the sixth evening, a U.N. committee was trying to formulate a demand for an explanation.

And I realized with a jolt that we'd been here almost a week and were two days into a new month and nothing visible had been accomplished—except that a lot of people were getting nervous. "Do you realize how long we've been here?" I said suddenly. "And how little has been done?"

Danni shrugged, barely looking up from her section of the paper. Laurie was stretched out on the floor; Tweedlioop was off in his "cave." "You're not surprised, are you? I told you this was likely."

"Yes, I know. And you know I don't blame *you* for any of it." I had, a little, the first day we were brought here and found out we weren't going to be leaving. I'd wanted to know why she hadn't tried to invoke some legal angle to let us keep Tweedlioop at home. She'd quietly explained that that wouldn't work, it would waste time and would interfere with our main objective: to help him get home. If anybody could do anything about it, it was Giannelli—so we'd have to play his game for a while.

"But it's been so *long!*" I said. "While we dillydally, they might leave—if they're out there at all. They may have already left."

"True enough. But you can only rush these things so much. Believe me, Bill, we're pushing as hard as we dare." She laid the paper down in her lap. "Do you remember the first night I was in Florida, when I said I might not be able to do much for you as a lawyer?"

"Yes." It was only a week ago, though it seemed much

longer. "I don't hold that against you, Danni. I know it's not your fault."

"On the contrary," she said, sounding surprisingly cheerful, "I'm not out of the game yet. Knowledge of the law is only half a lawyer's arsenal, and not always even the most important part. They haven't given me much chance to use that, but I still have the other part."

"Which is?"

"I read people, and watch for ways to use what they think and feel—and things they're planning to use against me and my client. That I can still do, and I tell you we still have a chance. Not as good as we'd like, but we'll blow even that if we push too hard too soon. Giannelli's anxious, but cautious."

When she said a lawyer read people, I wondered whether she read me—and if so, what she read. But I didn't have the nerve to ask. Nor could I ask her to elaborate on exactly what she'd read in Giannelli, and how. Glumly, I picked my paper back up. "Communication's what's got us hung up. We're groping in the dark. They keep trying to guess what Tweedlioop is and what he means. If only we could talk to him!"

I turned a page, but before I could resume reading, Laurie lifted her head and said, "*I* can."

My first reaction was to shrug it off, but then something made me lay the paper back down and look right at her. "What?"

"I can talk to Tweedlioop."

Danni looked at her, too. "Of course you do, Laurie. We've heard you. But we're talking about *real* talk, where you tell him things and he understands and answers back and you understand his answers."

"So am I," said Laurie. "We do that."

Danni and I looked at each other. I wasn't about to open my mouth; my look probably said, *She's your daughter.* Danni said, "If that's true, why didn't you say anything about it before?"

"I did, the first time we met Mr. Giannelli. He didn't seem interested." She paused, then smiled. "Besides, we couldn't do it very well then. We were just starting to learn. But we've been practicing a lot this week. Tweedlioop gets *so* exasperated with those scientists. He says he can hardly wait to get back here and have some sensible conversation."

Danni shot me another look. I was inclined to dismiss the whole thing as childish imagination—but I was also inclined to grasp at anything that looked as if it had the slightest chance. "How can you talk to each other without a language you both speak? You speak good English, Laurie, but you can't make those twittery noises, and I don't think he can make anything else."

"Of course not," said Laurie, very patiently. "So what? He twitters and shows me what the twitters mean. I talk my way and show him what *I* mean. We each talk the way we can, and the other learns how to listen. What could be simpler than that?"

What indeed? I felt the beginnings of an odd excitement, and saw that Danni felt it, too. I recalled my earlier thought about how they might have the best chance of communication because of their shared immaturity, and realized that I should have taken it more seriously. My Russian professor in college claimed children under nine could usually learn a foreign language without an accent, while adults seldom could. Among humans, at least, children have fewer cultural biases and set ways of thinking, at every level, than adults. I suspected that was true among Tweedlioop's people as well.

Adults might spend years trying to construct a speakable *lingua franca*. Leave it to two kids to cut right to the heart of the matter and just start using *both* languages that either of them already spoke!

I found myself envying their flexibility, which I must once have had, too. More important, I found myself hatching a scheme to *use* it—

If it was true.

"Can you show us how you and Tweedlioop talk?" I asked, trying to restrain my enthusiasm.

"I think he's sleeping," she said.

"Wake him. It's important, Laurie. Can you call him from here and tell him to come out? Tell him I have an idea about how to contact his folks."

"Well . . . okay." She got up and opened the door to the next room. "Tweedlioop," she called softly into the darkness. "Please come here. Bill wants to talk. He has an idea." Pause. "Tweedlioop?"

Brief twitters and flutings came from the darkness. Laurie came back and sat cross-legged on the floor. "He'll be here soon," she said. "Don't expect us to talk about fancy things. Remember we're still learning. We both miss a lot."

It wouldn't have taken much to impress me. I felt myself jump and lean forward when Tweedlioop ambled into the room twenty seconds later and crawled up on Laurie's knee. He twittered.

"Sorry to wake you," Laurie told him. "But Bill wants to see us talk. He says it's very important."

Tweedlioop piped some more. Laurie frowned. "I

missed a lot of that. Sorry. Let's go on. Can you show me where Bill is?"

Tweedlioop hesitated slightly, then stretched a paw toward me.

"Yes. And where's Mommy?" Tweedlioop pointed. "Very good. Go to Mommy, get the newspaper, and take it to Bill. Please." Pause. Tweedlioop twittered. "Yes, I know it's silly. She could take it to him or he could go get it. It's just to show them that you understand. Please, Tweedlioop. For me."

Tweedlioop hesitated just a second longer, then scampered over to Danni. She handed him a section of the paper and he dragged it across the floor to me. "Thank you, Tweedlioop!" I said, patting him lightly. Never before had I been so excited to get the sports section. I reached into my pocket. "How many coins do I have in my hand, Tweedlioop? Tell me and they're yours."

He looked around uncertainly, first at me, then at Laurie. He chirped and fluted. Laurie said, "He can't understand you very well. I think your voice is too different. I think he has trouble hearing low sounds." She addressed Tweedlioop, speaking carefully but avoiding gestures. "Go to Bill. He'll show you some round metal pieces. Count them. Then come back and tell me how many."

That was all he needed. He came back. I extended a hand filled with coins; I think I saw it shaking. I held it so he could see it but Laurie couldn't. He studied it briefly, then scampered back to Laurie and emitted a single, terse thrush-like phrase.

"Eleven," Laurie said confidently.

I counted, twice, and broke into an enormous grin. "By George," I breathed, "I think they've got it!"

We ran through a few more demonstrations, increasingly sophisticated, and then I suggested that Laurie send Tweedlioop back to bed with my heartfelt thanks.

He went. And I swooped down and hugged Laurie. "I have an idea," I declaimed. "But I have to talk it over with Giannelli first. Right away." I headed for the door, but paused before opening it. "Laurie," I asked, "did you happen to find out what 'Tweedlioop' really means?"

"Uh-huh. It means, 'I need help.' But he said we can still call him that."

Giannelli was in his quarters, trying to catch a few rare moments of relaxation, but I had little trouble convincing his night secretary that I was worth talking to. Giannelli met me in his office ten minutes later, himself in shirt-sleeves and the office *sans* banquet table. He looked tired. He motioned me without ceremony to a chair near the desk. "Now, what's all this about?"

"I think I have an answer to *how,*" I said. "I realize you're still working on *whether,* but I thought I should throw this in the hopper right away."

"I appreciate that. Okay, let's hear it. No, wait. Let me get Goodmill in here. May save time."

Goodmill, Giannelli's chief military advisor, showed up five minutes later in an outfit that might have been some version of either a military uniform or a business suit. Giannelli motioned him to another chair and said, "Mr. Nordstrom tells me he has an idea for contacting the aliens."

Goodmill, a dour and jowly fellow who could never quite erase a six-o'clock shadow, said, "We haven't settled the question of whether we should try that yet."

"Can't hurt to listen," said Giannelli. "The method may affect our decision. A letter with no return address and a misleading postmark is one thing; a meeting in a dark alley is something else. What did you have in mind, Bill?"

"We've been operating under a wrong assumption," I said. "We've been assuming we need a language we can both speak. But it's not really necessary. I can think of at least two situations in which two beings can communicate without a shared language."

Both leaders of our country stared at me with blank annoyance for a couple of seconds. Then Giannelli said, "One of them, I assume, is when they share not a language, but a translator. Unfortunately, we're not in that position."

"Maybe we're not," I said, "but maybe they are. We wouldn't know without trying. On the other hand, we may be closer than you think—because of my other possibility."

Goodmill glanced at his watch. "It's late," he observed. "I'd appreciate it if you'd come to the point."

"The other possibility," I said, "is that each speaker can *understand* the other's language. It doesn't matter if he can speak it. Speaking and understanding are two distinct skills. It's quite possible to have one without the other."

Goodmill was making no attempt to hide his annoyance; I must have interrupted his dinner. "Need I point out that we've had a team of experts hard at work for almost a week and we still don't have even *one* of those skills?"

"The trouble with experts," I said, "is that they know too much about How the Job Should Be Done. That's fine, if it's an old familiar job, but it can be a handicap if it's something really new." To soften the blow to adult pride, I outlined my theory of why a bright kid might make a better alien-interpreter-trainee than a team of adult experts. "While they've been studying away," I concluded, "Tweedlioop has spent a lot of spare time with Laurie, my attorney's nine-year-old daughter. They've made quite a bit of headway at talking to each other. Together, they could be a two-stage translator."

Giannelli and Goodmill looked at each other, then at me. "You have only Laurie's word for this?" Giannelli asked. "Or have you seen proof?"

"I've seen demonstrations," I said. "I was impressed. My proposal is this. Let Tweedlioop talk to the aliens. Rig a radiophone to broadcast from one of the big scope dishes, let Laurie tell Tweedlioop what we want him to do, and turn him loose."

Goodmill scowled. "And how do we know they're not plotting something right under our noses?"

"We're right there, and so is Laurie. She monitors what he says and lets us know about anything suspicious. Besides, he *is* just a kid, General. I doubt he's up to interstellar plotting."

"Even if you're right," said Goodmill, "kids can be used without their knowledge. I could tell you stories from our own history. . . . But I don't think I will." He took out a pipe and started tamping a sweet-smelling tobacco into it. "Frankly, I'm astonished that we're sitting here seriously discussing putting the fate of mankind into the hands of a child."

"*Two* children," I said. "The aliens are in the same boat."

"If they're there at all," said Giannelli. "We still don't know that."

"The sky searches haven't turned anything up?"

"Not yet. Haven't you asked Tweedlioop if they're still out there?"

I wasn't sure whether he was being sarcastic. "Not yet. I just found out he could talk to Laurie this evening. And I didn't want to get his hopes up if you're not willing to let him try. But he told me they were there before, and he still acts like he's hoping for help. I'd guess if you let him talk and sweep the ecliptic with his message, they'll hear him. Maybe we haven't seen them because they're hiding. But I'll bet they're listening."

Goodmill, scowling and puffing away on his pipe, didn't say anything. Neither did Giannelli, for a while. Then: "It's an interesting idea, Bill. Worth investigating, but I can't promise you anything. I'm sure you understand that General Goodmill's concerns can't be taken lightly. We'll have to make our own verification of Laurie's ability to converse with Tweedlioop, and if that pans out we'll have to determine from him whether your idea's worth trying. If it gets that far, then we'll consider your proposal in the light of the General's questions. That will require more closed sessions." He smiled apologetically. "So I'm afraid that's all I can tell you tonight—except thanks for coming."

More waiting; more frustration. Now Laurie was gone with Tweedlioop during the days, leaving Danni and me to fend for ourselves with time on our hands and our work far away. I think Danni was a little annoyed, at first, that I had taken my idea to Giannelli without discussing it with her first. But she quickly forgot that as she realized that

Laurie had no objection and the scheme had a chance of working. During the days we both read a lot, and sometimes we went for walks or sat on the porch. We talked about things we'd done and things we thought, and it turned out that her interests and experiences and values had even more points of contact with mine than I'd already seen. Even more, she had an unquenchable zest for life—and some of that, very gradually, rubbed off on me. For that I was most grateful.

Sometimes we kept to ourselves, not talking at all. Some of those times I wanted to ask her what she was thinking, but was afraid to. I knew she felt frustrated about being able to do so little here, and about being cut off from her Alaskan clients. I felt guilty about having gotten her into such a situation.

Why had I asked her to come?

Why had she agreed?

Laurie and Tweedlioop came home each evening tired, in highly variable moods. Danni and I tried to ask them what had happened, and increasingly Tweedlioop tried, through Laurie, to participate in telling us. But we couldn't get much coherent detail. The only pattern we saw was that Tweedlioop, despite occasional frustration, was increasingly excited—for they had told him, in very general terms, what they were considering.

But they had also told him it was "conditional" on the outcome of their tests with him and Laurie—and "other things." Still no word came of the closed hearings, and Danni and I began to worry that Tweedlioop was being built up for another crushing disappointment. She made some discreet efforts to find out what was going on behind closed doors, but to no avail.

After a week, Tweedlioop and Laurie started coming

home early, and after two more days the tests stopped altogether. Again all four of us were home all day, with time to kill and still in the dark. I tried to talk with Tweedlioop, to get to know him, but again he became withdrawn. We all started getting edgy. Sometimes we clashed and were glad our quarters were big enough to get away from one another. Danni became a little pushier in her quest for a progress report. Always she was quietly but firmly told that we would be informed when a decision was reached.

And finally it came. Giannelli summoned Danni and me to his office and showed us to chairs. Goodmill was there, too, and both of them wore curiously unreadable expressions. Giannelli wasted a few minutes telling us what we already knew about the plan I had proposed and the implications he and his advisors had been pondering. All very sober, dull stuff.

And then, to our astonishment, he smiled broadly. "So let me come to the point. The upshot of all this is that after carefully weighing all these factors, we've decided this gesture would be a splendid thing for us to do. Preparations are already under way, and we hope that very soon Tweedlioop will be safely on his way home—wherever that may be."

And before we could react, Giannelli and Goodmill were on their feet and headed for the door. Goodmill, beaming no less broadly than Giannelli, clapped Danni on the shoulder and boomed, "Congratulations, Ms. O'Millian. That's a fine daughter you've raised and a fine thing she's doing. You should be proud of her."

"WHAT BOTHERS ME," DANNI SAID WHEN WE WERE back in our quarters, "is that they're *too* enthusiastic now. I can't help wondering just what went on in those meetings to change their minds."

"Me too," I said. "I may be too suspicious, but I can't quite believe it's just the goodness of their hearts."

"You're not too suspicious, but let's not dwell on that now. For now, let's just be glad it's being tried. If the results are right, the motives may not matter."

"I guess you're right. Come on, I want to tell Tweedlioop the news."

I could hear him and Laurie talking quietly behind her closed door, with long pauses. I knocked lightly. "Who is it?" Laurie called.

"It's us," I said. "We have news for Tweedlioop. May we come in?"

Little-girl talk, too quiet to understand, then a twitter, then, "Sure. The door's unlocked."

I felt a little like an intruder. Laurie was stretched out on her stomach on the semi-made bed, chin resting on folded arms and looking up at Tweedlioop. He was perched on the nearest corner of the dresser. The only chair was covered with stray clothes of Laurie's. Danni sat there; I lowered myself to a corner of the bed after asking Laurie whether she minded.

"Sorry to interrupt," I said, "but we've been talking to Mr. Giannelli and General Goodmill, and you'll want to know what they said. They want to try to send Tweedlioop home. They want him to try to call his people's ship on the radio. He can talk to them, and you and he can be interpreters so their leaders can talk to ours."

Laurie seemed unimpressed and didn't bother to translate. "He knows that," she said. "They hinted at it several times while they were giving us their silly tests. But he doesn't believe they really mean it. Neither do I."

"But they do," I said. "That's the whole point. They've decided to go through with it. The tests were to convince them it might work; the closed meetings were to convince them they dared. The generals are afraid, Laurie. But they're going to do it anyway."

"Hmph!" she sniffed. She looked up at me with wide eyes in which hope and distrust struggled for dominance. "Really?" she said cautiously. "You wouldn't kid us?"

"Not about that. Of course, we're not sure it will work—"

But Laurie had already released her pent-up reserves of feeling and was no longer listening. "*Yahoo!*" she shrieked, and then she was sitting up, leaning forward so her face was close to Tweedlioop's. "They're going to let you do it, Tweedlioop! They're going to let you call your people!"

His excitement was not immediate. He queried her with brief chirpings. Her replies were a mixture of English and unhuman sounds I'd never heard her make before, evidently fragments she'd picked up in imitation of his language. But after a few of those, he erupted in a torrent of excited jabber far beyond anything I'd heard from him yet. He lunged into Laurie's lap and climbed up on her shoulder, nuzzling her cheek and ear. She rubbed him, and before long we were all laughing and hugging each other, momentarily forgetting it was not yet time to count chickens.

Tweedlioop was the first to remember. As suddenly as it had begun, his gleeful outpouring stopped. He crouched between Laurie's pillow and the headboard, now silent, shaking as rapidly as he had that day in Alaska when he'd seen the plane flying over. Laurie bent over him, alarmed. "Tweedlioop! What's wrong?"

He fluted almost inaudibly. "He's afraid," Laurie said.

"Afraid?" Danni echoed. "Of what?"

Laurie whispered to him, interspersing more humanized chirps among the words. They talked back and forth for a while and then she said, "He says he can't tell us."

Danni and I looked at each other for signs of understanding. I said, "Is he afraid they won't still be there?"

More Laurie and Tweedlioop talk. "He says a little. But he says maybe he's even more afraid that they will."

I felt my forehead crease. "What's that supposed to mean?"

They talked some more. "He says he can't explain. But he seems afraid of what the others will say or do when he meets them."

"Oh." It didn't fit. Why should Tweedlioop be afraid to see the folks he'd seemingly been so eager to rejoin ever since I met him?

Could Tweedlioop be some sort of criminal?

I couldn't believe it, emotionally—but I couldn't rule it out, intellectually. We'd been trying to learn who he was and why he was here, but the language barrier was still pretty high. And there were some areas which he just didn't seem to want to talk about. . . .

I tried to ignore it, but I knew the jarring possibility would continue to haunt me. No matter: I knew where I stood—right behind Tweedlioop, wherever that might be. I asked, "Has he changed his mind? Would he rather *not* try to contact them?"

A very brief exchange, then, "No. He's glad to have the chance. He says he has to do it, afraid or not—and he's only thought of the worries since the chance became real."

How well I knew that feeling. (Doesn't every human?) I looked at our mysterious little friend with a mixture of admiration for what seemed to be courage, and a nagging curiosity about what wasn't showing.

Then I said, "Okay. They want to get started right away. There are a lot of details to work out. . . ."

Again time passed—but not too much. It took awhile to arrange things, but for the first time, for whatever reason, there was a sense of urgency in the air—a sense that things were finally *happening*.

The government, not surprisingly, didn't reveal many details of the plan, even to us. But I picked up inklings from Giannelli, who remained superficially friendly though tight-lipped, and from Laurie, who went with Tweedlioop to several briefing sessions.

I wish I could have gone to those myself. From what I could gather, they were trying to ascertain from Tweedlioop, through Laurie, that the aliens used electromagnetic communication, and to get an idea what frequencies and what kinds of modulation they used. It was an interesting challenge, because Laurie knew very little of such things; and while Tweedlioop knew some, he did not describe them in terms much like ours.

Even so, they managed to narrow the field. Amplitude modulation seemed to be out, but they could only guess what bandwidths were used for FM. Nor did they have much idea what bands to use, though Tweedlioop seemed to hint that his folks would be scanning several. Giannelli looked preoccupied when he told me that, and I thought I knew why. If Tweedlioop was really just a little lost kid, why would they go to all that trouble for him?

Would he even be here in the first place?

Well, we'd find out soon enough.

Maybe.

Technicians worked day and night to rig the electronics that would do the work. We—I use the term loosely—would broadcast from here (wherever "here" was), but the signal would be piped by shielded underground phone cables to the National Radio Astronomy Observatory at Green Bank, West Virginia. That was where it would leave Earth, flung heavenward by the 140-foot steerable dish while a couple of the interferometer scopes—with backups around the world—listened for replies.

The idea was that Green Bank, in addition to being well equipped for the job, was close enough to our hideout to facilitate transfers, yet far enough so that any alien craft enticed in by our broadcasts would not endanger Giannelli and the other Important People here. Green Bank was where they would come, if they came at all. Those coordinates were being transmitted; our funny little village wouldn't even be mentioned. And if they had the technology we suspected they did, the incoming visitors would likely trace the signal for themselves, right back to the big dish nestled in its valley.

Where they would be met by a welcoming committee which, I gathered, would include an imposing array of heavy armaments poised for action—and vehicles to bring the visitors here.

The nature of the welcoming committee bothered me. Giannelli told me about it privately, and I kept it to myself —though I was pretty sure Danni, at least, had anticipated it. He explained his reasons for handling it that way, and I couldn't really argue with them. But the idea still bothered me.

The hours ticked by, too full of preparations to leave much time for worry.

And then The Hour was at hand.

The broadcast took place on Sunday, four days after I broached the idea to Giannelli. Or rather, the first transmission and taping happened then. After that, we kept reminding ourselves, we had to expect a long, anticlimactic wait as the taped message was broadcast over and over on many frequencies and in many ways, hoping that one of them would be heard by the right listeners and none by anyone else.

That was a touchy business, of course, but measures could be taken to cut the risk way down. The very nature of the dish helped: the "broadcast" was confined to a rather tight beam, trading sky coverage for punch. That was one reason the wait for an answer might be so long

—the message would have to be repeated not only on many frequencies, but in many directions, with the hope that one of them might eventually connect. They could be timed to avoid interception by any known communication satellite or spacecraft. A standard mechanism existed, which wouldn't look *too* suspicious if justified in terms of "delicate observations," for keeping aircraft out of the zone near Green Bank where they might intercept the transmissions. There was still the slight chance that an unauthorized pilot would wander in despite the ban, and the still smaller chance that while doing so he would be listening to the frequency then in use (which would *never* be at or near any aviation frequency in use there). But that minimal risk would have to be accepted, unless Giannelli was prepared to go so far as shooting such wanderers down on sight—which I hoped he wasn't. There was no way to get a conversation going unless *somebody* made a first transmission, and we had been elected by default.

Danni and I were there, but solely as observers. Danni and I sat in the "control room," half of a room that looked like any small radio studio, our folding metal chairs surrounded by transmitting and recording equipment and two technicians who paid us little attention. Through a glass partition we saw the other half, a place of white acoustic tile and no furniture except a table, some folding chairs, and a cluster of microphones dangling from a boom. Laurie faced us across the table, neatly scrubbed and dressed and nervous. She kept stroking Tweedlioop, who skittered around on the table in front of her, his head dwarfed by the mike he was to use. Giannelli and Goodmill faced each other from the ends of the table. After a while, one of the technicians, behind us but faintly mirrored in the window, said, "Ready when you are, Mr. President."

Giannelli's voice came from a speaker behind us. "Ready."

A switch clicked. "Recording and broadcasting, sir."

I glanced sideways at Danni. Somehow it made me feel better to see that she looked tense, too. We had known that they were going to make the first transmission live while taping it in Green Bank for prompt rebroadcast and here as a backup. We did not know what they were going to say. Laurie and Tweedlioop had been brought here two hours earlier to run through the script; Danni and I were not invited.

"Greetings from Earth," Giannelli began, and I noticed that for once even he looked self-conscious. "This is Wilbur Giannelli, President of the United States of America. I don't know who you are or whether you can understand this. But in case you can, I want to tell you that we know you're there and we look forward to a friendly and peaceful meeting with you. One of you is here with us; we call him Tweedlioop. He is safe and well and looks forward to rejoining you. But let him speak for himself."

He stopped and seconds ticked by. "Laurie?" he prompted.

She jumped. "Oh. I'm sorry. Tweedlioop, it's time for you to talk. Right into the mike."

Danni's hand squeezed mine and didn't let go. Tweedlioop started out haltingly, quietly—almost timidly. At first Laurie tried to whisper running translations to Giannelli, but soon gave it up. I suspected Tweedlioop was being more colloquial and idiomatic now than he ever was with her, and once he got going he gradually picked up steam.

142

Ever faster and more animated grew his outpourings—except occasionally he seemed to catch on something and pause, briefly unable to continue. There was no waiting for replies, of course; if his listeners were where he'd seemed to say, one radio exchange would take at least eleven hours. We couldn't understand what he was saying, but we could make guesses about what was happening in those apparently emotional pauses. All we had to do was imagine Laurie in his situation, trying to call us, not knowing for sure whether we were even that close.

Finally he was finished. He lay on the table, motionless except for heavy breathing. We felt as drained as he looked, as if we'd been through it all with him.

For several seconds, silence reigned. Laurie stroked him lightly, looking much too solemn for a nine-year-old. Finally Giannelli asked her, "Can you tell us what he said?"

She looked at Giannelli with an expression I couldn't quite read. "The things you'd say in his position," she said. "I can't tell you much more. He's safe; he misses them; he hopes they'll come to take him home." A long pause. "There was more, but I couldn't understand all of it. He used words I don't know, and some of it was too fast." Another pause. "And some of it was too personal."

Giannelli nodded. "I think I understand." But after a judicious wait he added, "Anything that Mr. Goodmill needs to know about?"

This time I could read her expression: the scorn was unmistakable. "Of course not."

"Good," said Giannelli. "Then let's do the last part. Ready to translate for me?"

Laurie nodded gravely.

"Good girl." Giannelli again became the orator. "Our

great nation is as eager to help Tweedlioop rejoin you as you are to have him back."

Laurie leaned close to the furry ambassador from the stars. "Time to translate, Tweedlioop. Tell them the President said . . ." She repeated his words verbatim, but at a pitch and with a delivery better attuned to his ears. Tweedlioop twittered and stopped.

"We regret," Giannelli went on, "that we cannot bring him out to you ourselves." Laurie translated; Tweedlioop translated again. I wondered how much got through. "We can, however, tell you how to meet us to pick him up here. This signal is coming to you from a valley containing several large white parabolic antennas. . . ."

Piece by piece, Giannelli spelled out directions to Green Bank, including everything from latitude and longitude—referred to easily recognizable landmarks—to a detailed description of the Appalachian valley and its radiotelescope array. It took a long time. There were a lot of details that had to be included, and each had to be relayed through Laurie and Tweedlioop—one or both of whom sometimes lacked the needed words.

But finally it was done, and we all dispersed without further ado to wait—yet again. The next day and a half was pervaded by an odd feeling of letdown. After all that buildup, the deed was done, and nothing visible happened —except that I knew the artillery at Green Bank was fully mobilized, and from time to time I found myself fervently hoping that they would have the good sense not to do anything rash if anybody actually came in.

But nobody came, and no radio signals were detected to suggest that anyone had heard ours. Twelve hours passed, and each additional one made it a little harder to believe that help was on the way. I knew our message was still going out, over and over, on frequency after frequency. But I increasingly feared that we, with all our good intentions, had played Tweedlioop as cruel a joke as any I'd imagined on my blackest night of indecision in Alaska.

Maybe I *should* have left him there.

Tuesday morning, at an obscenely early hour, I was dragged from fitful sleep by an insistent pounding on the door and buzzing of the intercom. I stumbled through the darkness to see what fool was making the racket, hoping to stop him before he woke Danni and Laurie.

I looked through the peephole, frowned, and opened the door. The technicians who had taken Tweedlioop to "school" were there, with an augmented guard of three soldiers armed to the teeth. Before I could open my mouth, their leader, overburdened with chevrons and rockers, said, "Sorry to disturb you at this hour, Mr. Nordstrom. We have orders to take Tweedlioop into custody. The President considers it necessary so we can present a united front and bargain from a strong position."

I felt my frown deepen, though I was still struggling to assimilate the words. "Why's it necessary?" I said thickly. "And couldn't it wait until morning?"

"You don't understand," said the military man. "They're here."

"*Who's* here?" I snapped irritably—and then the first glimmer of understanding got through. But I couldn't believe . . . "You mean the aliens have landed at Green Bank already?"

"No," said the soldier. "Not at Green Bank. *Here.*"

IX

I THINK I WAS AS SURPRISED AND CURIOUS AS ANY-
body at their time, place, and mode of arrival, but I failed
to see the need for hauling Tweedlioop off under heavy
guard in the middle of the night. (I never claimed to be
politically astute.) So as soon as the hour was slightly less
obscene, Danni and I bulled our way in to see Giannelli
and demand an explanation.

"Please sit down," he said, motioning us to a pair of
chairs with the same fatherly unflappability that had won
his election and kept him popular. "I don't like this any
more than you do. It was a matter of simple necessity. We
have no intention of holding Tweedlioop prisoner or anything like that—but until we make sure his rescuers are
peaceable, we have to have some bargaining leverage in
case we need it. So we talk first and turn him over just a
little later. If they're what you think they are, there should
be no problem."

For a few seconds neither of us said anything. Then
Danni asked quietly, "What do *you* think they are, Mr.
Giannelli?"

"I don't know," said the President. "But if they're not

146

friends, we don't want them for enemies. Have you thought about what they've done here?" I had, but I didn't interrupt. "They've taken less than two days—tops—to come in from wherever they were—assuming they came in response to our signal. That's impressive anywhere they could have been, and awesome if they were where we thought they were. We don't *know* where they were because they slipped right through the concerted efforts of our best detection systems without a trace. And they came *here,* not to Green Bank. Do you know what that means? They must have somehow traced our very first transmission back here through the wire from Green Bank." He looked troubled, but not quite as troubled as I later thought he should. "We'd give a lot to be able to do any *one* of those things!" He changed the subject abruptly. "Would you like to see their vehicle?"

I certainly would, I assured him. He stood up and led us out of the room, through a maze of corridors, and up a camouflaged elevator to the surface. It was nice to be outside again: for some reason we hadn't gone out much the last few days. It was a crisp, clear morning, with dew sparkling on artistically lit grass. A slight chill and scattered touches of color among the trees hinted at the approach of autumn.

Giannelli led us through the woods on the red chip path that connected the "town" to the airstrip. A new building had appeared near one end of the runway, looking a lot like one of those prefab backyard sheds from Sears—or possibly a small, hastily erected garage. An old man with a hunting license and a shotgun strolled nearby; I suspected neither he nor his shotgun was quite what it seemed.

Giannelli unlocked a door and Danni and I followed him into the new shed. He flicked a switch, and a couple of bare incandescent bulbs flooded the interior with light. It looked like nothing so much as a suburban garage—but the thing in the middle didn't look much like the Average American Car.

"Look familiar?" Giannelli asked.

It certainly did. It was the twin of the one Danni and I had seen on that hillside in Alaska last month, but without the infirmities. It had the same metallic-plastic orange skin, the same bits of protruding detail that I had seen but not consciously noted—but no ugly gash and no apparent corpses.

Its size—or lack of it—hit me just as hard now as before. And there was a faint smell about it—quite different from the one I remembered from Alaska, but no less alien. That one had been the smell of alien death; this one, I felt just as sure, was that of machinery recently used. This, I reminded myself, was a thing which just last night had brought intelligent beings here from the stars—and in which they planned to return.

I was no less awed than when I had viewed the wreck with Tweedlioop—and I could see that Danni wasn't either. I finally found my tongue and asked, "How did you get it in here?"

"We didn't," said Giannelli. "They landed it out in the open and then got out and came in to see us. We didn't think it would do to leave it standing out, and we were afraid to try moving it. So we built the shed around it."

"They didn't try to stop you?"

Giannelli shook his head. "Once they got out, they didn't seem to give it another thought."

I considered what that might mean. That they were too naive to realize what humans might try to do?

Or that they were so confident of their superiority that we were not worth worrying about?

I tried not to think too hard about possible answers until I had some basis for my conjectures. "Hm-m-m," I said. "Where are they now?"

"The chucks? We've offered them quarters and they moved right in. They wanted to rest, but we'll be meeting to talk this afternoon. You're invited, of course."

Seldom had I heard a statement so casually loaded with narrative hooks. *Chucks?* Presumably that was a nickname the few humans who'd seen them had already given the aliens. Hardly surprising, if they looked anything like the ones I'd seen in the wreck. They looked as much like woodchucks or rockchucks as anything else earthly, and humans are quick to seize on things like that—and to hide fears with familiarity.

Somehow they'd already set up a meeting for this afternoon—"to talk." An innocent enough statement—except that it implied that they were *able* to talk to humans, and in fact some talk had already taken place. Giannelli refused to tell us more: he said we'd find out soon enough. So we resigned ourselves to waiting.

The ironic part was that we were invited and Tweedlioop wasn't. True, we were not full participants. Laurie was to act as "corroborating interpreter" if needed, and Danni and I were told quite bluntly that we were not to speak unless spoken to. But Tweedlioop wasn't there at all, and he had more at stake than anyone.

Needless to say, the chucks noticed, too. They were

already in the conference room when we arrived, sitting on their haunches like prairie dogs on sentry duty in the middle of the oval mahogany table. Both looked like the one I had compared to a large marmot when I saw the bodies in Tweedlioop's wrecked shuttle. Maybe it was just as well that they hadn't sent any who looked like wolverines; people do react to appearances. Alive, these looked bright and alert and somehow grandfatherly. Their fur was sleek and well groomed, and the greenish tinge more vivid than in the corpses. Neither of them seemed to wear clothes, but one had a small blue-black disk held at his throat by a collar. (His? I had no idea what gender they were, though I guessed that both were the same. But I have to call them something.)

We humans took seats around the table: Giannelli, Goodmill, Laurie, Danni, and me. It struck me as odd and disturbing that the only advisor the President had brought with him was a military one—in full regalia—but I didn't have much time to think about it. As soon as we were all seated, the chuck with the throat disk twittered, in a way similar to Tweedlioop's but perhaps half an octave lower.

And the throat disk said, in a peculiar hybrid of British and American radio-announcer English, "Where is Tweedlioop?"

"He is safe," said Giannelli, and the alien's throat disk twittered softly. In an aside to Danni and me he explained, "Apparently they've been studying us remotely for quite some time. They already had an operational translator when they arrived. That will make it easier—though I still want Laurie to let us know immediately if she questions any of its translations." He turned back to the chuck spokesman—let's call him the Ambassador. "Tweedlioop will be reunited with you shortly. But this is such a momentous occasion—the first meeting of two intelligent and civilized species from different worlds—we thought it appropriate that we adults meet first to discuss the possible benefits of this contact for both—"

The chuck without a throat disk made a peculiar spasmodic noise; it remained untranslated, so we could only guess what it meant. I wasn't sure I liked my guess. Giannelli went on, "We are impressed by what little we have seen of your civilization, and honored to have had the opportunity to care for a member of it. Clearly you have concepts and abilities which we lack; no doubt we have some which we could share with you. Surely it would be to our common benefit to compare—"

"There is no reason," the Ambassador interrupted with a twitch of long whiskers, "for Tweedlioop not to be present while we discuss such matters—*if* we discuss such matters."

Goodmill frowned. Giannelli seemed momentarily taken aback. "I apologize for our error. We mistakenly assumed that a child would not be interested in such things. Tweedlioop is a child—an immature member of your species—is he not?"

The Ambassador did not answer right away. His companion—let's call him the Silent Partner—was apparently not equipped or expected to participate in the main conversation, and spent most of his time sitting motionless except for an occasional twitch of his whiskers. I had no idea what his function was. Eventually the Ambassador said, "Yes. But if you assumed that a child would not be interested in the matters you hoped to discuss, why did you bring one of your own?" He gestured toward Laurie with a small two-thumbed hand, similar to Tweedlioop's but with the fingers thinner and more efficient-looking.

Again Giannelli seemed a tad startled, as if he hadn't expected them to recognize Laurie as a child. But he recovered quickly. "She is not an extremely young child, and she is our best translator of your language, due to a special gift for such things. We did not realize you would bring your own."

The Ambassador made a noise similar to the one I had earlier guessed might be laughter; the translator ignored it. "But since we did, your child's skills are not required, are they?"

"Perhaps not. Nevertheless, we prefer to keep her here. Translation is a subtle process. It is to both our advantages to have two opinions."

"As you wish." The Ambassador's fur rippled oddly, a ringlike wave sweeping his fur from neck to a final twitch of his vestigial tail. "It doesn't matter to us. Besides, she's probably more interested than you realize—as is Tweedlioop." He addressed Laurie directly. "I hate to keep referring to you as if you weren't here, my child. Do you have a name?"

Laurie looked startled. "Yes," she said hesitantly. "Laurie. Laurie O'Millian."

The Ambassador touched his chest with his hand; so did the Silent Partner. "We are honored to meet you, Laurie O'Millian." He turned back to the President. "Your mistake is easily understood and easily remedied. Please bring Tweedlioop here now."

"I'm afraid," said Giannelli, "that's impossible."

A ruff of fur rose around the Ambassador's neck and

stayed there. "Why?" he asked, and somehow he managed to project a hint that he didn't believe it.

I didn't believe it either, but Giannelli unflinchingly said, "I'm sorry, but that's the way it is. Tweedlioop is safe and well guarded in a location nearby but not conveniently accessible from this room. You have my assurance that he will be delivered to you as soon as we've established where both of our peoples stand and what the conditions of the transfer are."

"Conditions?" said the Ambassador.

"Yes." Giannelli's jaw had taken a firm set. "Mr. Ambassador—if I may call you that—I think we may speak plainly to each other. Our peoples are from different worlds, but surely we share at least the desire for survival and prosperity and an awareness of the dangers which strangers can pose. If both our peoples are as civilized as I think they are, we will both recognize the need to establish to our mutual satisfaction that neither of us represents a threat to the other. I think I can point out without giving offense that from our point of view you might well appear to be intruders in our solar system and on our planet. Surely you will see the reasonableness of our wanting to know why you came here and what you intend to do."

The Ambassador stared, silent and motionless. I could see his breathing, considerably more rapid than a human's. Danni was frowning, but not as much as I. She must have anticipated more of this. I could see that Giannelli's question was legitimate and needed an answer, but it seemed to me that the way he was approaching it was unduly blunt, at least bordering on the reckless. We knew very little about these beings. If they took offense . . .

"You ask us," the Ambassador said slowly, "to accept

your assurance that Tweedlioop will be returned to us. Why should you not accept *our* assurance that our mission and intentions are private and harmless and will not affect you?"

"We would like to," said Giannelli, "but we can't afford to. There is too much more at stake."

"Not as much as you think," said the Ambassador.

I wondered what he meant by that, but Giannelli passed right over it. "Nevertheless, we need more concrete assurances. Furthermore, I would point out that despite our uncertainty about your intentions and the wisdom of contacting you, we did it, at considerable risk and expense and effort, for the sole purpose of returning Tweedlioop to you. We are eager to do so. But, to be quite frank, we think that what we have put into our goodwill gesture warrants some recognition on your part."

Danni's frown deepened, perhaps even surpassing mine. I'm sometimes a little slow to catch on to the subtleties of people's dealings, especially when the people are politicians and diplomats. I wasn't sure I really understood what was going on—and I didn't want to believe what it sounded like.

Again the Ambassador deliberated, that ruff still rigid on his neck. Finally he asked, "What do you want?"

Giannelli seemed to relax a bit, as if he'd won some small victory. "We are a young spacefaring race," he said amiably. "We have only recently begun to travel beyond our home planet. No doubt our methods and abilities seem primitive to you. Nonetheless, perhaps you remember, at least vicariously, that you too were once at this stage. We recognize that it is a critical one in our history. If we successfully complete our transition to a fully and routinely spacefaring people—in some modest sense like yours—our future is bright. If we do not do so soon, there is a danger that we will so deplete our resources that we will not be able to complete the transition at all. We will be trapped on a single planet, doomed to extracting a life of slowly diminishing quality from a slowly diminishing supply of resources."

The Ambassador inclined his head slightly. "Your perceptiveness is a good sign. Every intelligent race goes through such a dilemma, to a greater or lesser degree. Those that recognize the problem are more likely to solve it."

"Not all of us," Giannelli said carefully, "do recognize it. We were hoping that in return for what we have done for you, you might be persuaded to share some small portion of your knowledge that might make our successful completion of the transition more certain. The design and behavior of your landing craft, for example, indicate to us that you have more efficient ways of producing, distributing, and utilizing propulsive energy than we do. If we knew how to do those things, we could move more rapidly into space and accomplish more there with less drain on our limited planetary resources."

A lengthy silence. "And you want us to tell you these things?"

Giannelli nodded. "Any suggestions you can make would be profoundly appreciated."

This time there was no hesitation at all. "No," said the Ambassador. "I'm very sorry, but that's quite impossible."

A stunned look flashed across Giannelli's face, and then his mask fell back into place. "You needn't tell us everything," he said. "Even a hint or two, to point our researchers in the right directions—"

"Even that is impossible," said the Ambassador. "As you say, we have been spacefarers longer than you. This is not our first contact with a race at an earlier stage of development which sought our help. We have learned through painful experience to resist the temptation to give it."

"But . . . why?"

"Any action has side effects. The side effects are difficult to control, and usually regrettable—for the younger civilization." The Ambassador's face was oddly contorted and he spoke slowly, as if fighting remembered pain. "Your own planet is still polycultural. Your history must provide examples of the things we are speaking of."

Giannelli's face went blank and he didn't answer for a while. What was he thinking of? Amerindians? Polynesians? Eskimos? Myself, I'd read enough anthropology and science fiction so that the Ambassador's worries were not new to me. I wasn't sure he was right, that we would have to repeat the mistakes of our ancestors, that a mature culture helping a younger one had to destroy the younger.

But I wasn't sure he was wrong, either. And the decision, it seemed to me, was theirs, not ours.

Giannelli, when he finally spoke, seemed to echo my thoughts. "There have been problems between cultures here," he admitted. "But your civilization and ours are older and wiser than those involved. We can avoid their mistakes."

The Ambassador's head bobbed oddly. "That," he said solemnly, "is perhaps the most insidious trap of all. We ourselves have fallen into it too often. We shall not do so again. Ever."

Giannelli stared. "But . . . surely our case is special. I tried to explain earlier. We are at a crisis stage."

"So were we," said the Ambassador. "The problem of transition is one that every race must solve for itself. Even yours."

"But the risks," said Giannelli, regathering a portion of his composure, "fall upon us, not you. Surely it is our prerogative to take them upon ourselves, if we consider them preferable to the alternatives."

"No doubt," said the Ambassador. "But it is we who must decide whether to make the risks available to you. We choose not to. I'm sorry, but we cannot see it your way." He paused. "We are willing to assure you our original mission is entirely peaceful and does not concern you. Nevertheless, if it makes you uncomfortable, we will abort it and leave your system as soon as Tweedlioop is in our hands. You will have our profound gratitude, but there is nothing else we dare leave you. I'm sorry."

For a second or two longer Giannelli looked off balance, but then, with a shrug and a smile, he was himself again. "Well, let's not press that point now. Your assurance of peaceful intent will be helpful, but it will carry more weight if it's more specific. Whatever we decide, I'm going to have to answer to all my fellow humans when they ask one overwhelmingly important question. What are you doing here?"

The Ambassador twittered to the Silent Partner. His translator remained silent, but the Silent Partner did not. For at least a minute they talked, often with animated gestures and unreadable body language, including those peculiar ripplings of fur. Then he told Giannelli, "It would really be best for all of us if you'd quit harping on this question. We cannot divulge the information you request."

And there we were again. The conversation kept bumping from one impasse to another, and most of them were the same. This time Goodmill broke the silence. "Then perhaps we should bypass that one and ask you something else. Never mind why you are here. How many of you are there? There was the shuttle that crashed with Tweedlioop. You two came in another. Are there still more of you in orbit?"

"Perhaps," said the Ambassador. "Perhaps not."

Giannelli scowled almost imperceptibly. Goodmill ignored the non-answer and moved smoothly to his next question. "Why is Tweedlioop so important to you?"

"Our young are always important to us. Would you not react in a similar way if your young translator were stranded among us?" He gestured at Laurie.

Fear flashed across her face. She shot a wild glance at her mother. "Mommy, are they going to do something to me?"

Danni patted her arm. "No, Laurie. Don't worry." But even as she reassured her daughter, her face showed icy disdain for the diplomats before her. I couldn't tell which she distrusted more—ours or theirs.

Giannelli ignored all that. "Maybe," he said coolly, in answer to the Ambassador. "Maybe not. We also value our young—but other things also have values and costs, and sometimes they must be weighed against each other. Certainly we would *want* to rescue Laurie under those conditions, but the cost to the rest of us might be so high that we couldn't." I suspected he was talking too much, but I was too busy listening to think much about it. "We think even you must be subject to such considerations. To put it bluntly, we think there's a good deal more to Tweedlioop than you've told us. We think he has some special importance to you. Do you deny it?"

The Ambassador and the Silent Partner consulted. The Ambassador said, "No."

Giannelli waited a few seconds. "Are you going to explain?"

The Ambassador did not hesitate. "No."

With a barely perceptible sigh of impatience, Giannelli turned to Laurie. "Laurie, were you listening to what the Ambassador and his friend said?"

Laurie sat stiffly in her chair, staring straight ahead. "Yes."

"How much did you understand?"

"Some." She answered with obvious reluctance. "But I missed quite a bit."

"Would you tell us what you think you understood?"

She waited. "I missed a lot," she repeated—and then she burst into tears. "And I'm afraid!"

Giannelli stared at her, letting nothing show but a measured dose of sympathy—just enough to make his determination less forbidding. "There's nothing to be afraid of, Laurie. All I want you to do is tell us—"

"What we chose not to," the Ambassador interrupted. The ruff of fur stood very stiff around his neck. "We are disappointed, Mr. Giannelli, that you have so little regard for our feeble attempt at a private conversation under very awkward conditions. I fear it tells us things about your character that we would rather not have known. But I will not stand by and see you abuse your own young on our behalf. There's no need to put her on the spot." He stood up straight and drew a deep breath, letting it out with a long, low whistle. The ruff on his neck subsided and his fur became glossy smooth from head to tail. "I will tell you what you want to know." ·

He paused as if composing himself. The human spectators waited in heavy silence. When the Ambassador finally began his story, his face and body remained virtually motionless. His chirpings were slow and subdued, and the translator made his "voice" soft and careful. "We don't really understand your system of societal regulation," he said. "We have tried, but its complexity overwhelms us. Your culture seems fragmented into a vast hierarchy of levels and a bewildering multiplicity of units at each level. Each unit seems virtually independent of the others, and to our eyes most of the units seem to consist largely of individuals more concerned about personal gain than about ensuring the smooth and generally beneficial functioning of the whole.

"I hope you will forgive my bluntness; I do not wish to offend. But I think it necessary to preface my explanation of our mission with a description of how your approach to the problem looks to us. Perhaps that will help you to understand us, for I suspect our approach will sound quite as odd to you as yours does to us.

"I do not propose to say that either system has more validity than the other in any universal sense. It may be that each is ideally suited to its users, though we willingly concede that perhaps ours could be improved. Still, it has served us well for a very long time, and it is very different from yours.

"It long ago became apparent that the problems of various groups among us were so interrelated that we dared not treat them as independent. You might think that the fact that we are spread among many star systems would eliminate many of the problems of interaction. You might think, being as far as you are from even modest faster-than-light travel, that at least the planets would *have* to be essentially isolated from each other. I think you will learn otherwise much sooner than you think." He looked at the President. "If you, Mr. Giannelli, will recall your own reactions to our coming, you may get some inkling of how our technology has shrunk our portion of the galaxy, just as rapid communications and transportation have shrunk your planet and are beginning to shrink your solar system for you."

I could see that Giannelli was fighting a mighty itch to interrupt, but so far he was winning. He sat without a peep as the Ambassador went on: "We found that things functioned best for our people if the highest levels of decision-making were concentrated in a single individual."

At that Giannelli could contain himself no longer. "You're a dictatorship!" he gasped.

"Yes," the Ambassador said calmly, "in the strictly literal sense of the word. You are surprised."

"I . . . Yes. Forgive me, Your Excellency, but you were right. It does seem odd to us. I had assumed that . . . ah . . . a civilization so much older than ours would have evolved something better."

"And I hope," said the Ambassador, "you have not closed your mind to the possibility that we have. Please try to understand that our 'dictatorship' is a very different kind of thing from the ones that have plagued your history. Quite obviously, if his rule is to truly benefit the populace at large, our Ruler must be an extremely special individual. He must be intelligent, flexible, adaptable, impartial, well-informed, courageous, and many more things, all at a level most ordinary citizens find difficult even to conceive."

"On that," said Giannelli with a wry smile, "we can surely agree."

"Nonetheless," said the Ambassador, "such persons can exist. In general, they are made rather than born, and they are accorded the respect such people deserve for as long as they deserve it. I shall not attempt to describe to you all the mechanisms we have evolved to ensure that those chosen become fit Rulers and that they remain such and are treated as such. Part of it is faintly approximated by your phrase 'code of honor,' but we also emphasize a wide range of *competence* to a degree that you seemingly do not. For us, it works. Perhaps the most important difference in the way your dictators and ours come to power is that yours have always got there on their own initiative, driven by a kind of ambition that is the most absolute disqualification for ours."

"But even if you can find individuals with all these qualities," objected Goodmill, "your government would be very fragile. If you lose the individual who's in charge—"

"It does not happen often," said the Ambassador, "except from natural causes. That 'code of honor' has much to do with it. And there are always several alternates waiting to assume the Rule the instant it becomes necessary—and no sooner. Each of them is the product of a period of intensive training lasting approximately as long as your average lifespan. About a third of them eventually become Rulers."

Giannelli looked uncomfortable with the idea and impatient with the rambling. "This is all very interesting," he said, "but what does it have to do with—"

He broke off abruptly, a stunned look on his face. I think the answer hit all of us at once, and we all felt the same way. "Oh," Giannelli concluded in a very small voice.

The Ambassador's whole body seemed to relax; his fur seemed to soften and his upper torso swayed slowly from side to side. "Tweedlioop," he said, "is a Ruler-in-Reserve. He is very young and in the earliest stages of his training, but his potential is well established and the investment of time and resources in him is already considerable. Our visit to your solar system is simply part of his training. A Ruler must have learned by experience to cope with a very wide range of unfamiliar and dangerous situations. This was one of his first—he was to be deposited in a wild region of an alien planet where he would be left for a period to survive on his own in an alien ecology, with a small but finite possibility—which he was to avoid—of encountering intelligent natives." He made the "laughing" noise and added, "Due to the accident, that possibility is no longer as small as it was supposed to be. On behalf of all of us, I apologize most deeply for any distress and concern he has caused you."

He fell silent to let us absorb all this. So our little ball of fluff, Laurie's pet/playmate, was being groomed as an interstellar emperor. And he had, as I understood it, flunked one test—though I hoped due allowance would be made for its not being his fault.

Was that why he had been afraid of being rescued?

"Now that you understand," the Ambassador said presently, "I have no doubt that you'll recognize his extreme importance to us. Being as civilized a race as you are, naturally you will return him to us at once."

"We would like that very much," said Giannelli. "Unfortunately, as a race that has had to deal with others in the past, we must also fear for our own security. *And* we have a certain sense of fairness in dealings. We will gladly return him to you; we want your goodwill—and his, if he becomes your Ruler and we have further dealings with you."

"I'm afraid," the Ambassador said delicately, "that will not happen within your lifetime. We have already explained why that must be."

"Nevertheless, we wish to be assured of your goodwill when you leave—and that assurance will be far more convincing if accompanied by some concrete and meaningful gesture. A simple exchange of information, as we suggested earlier—"

"Is impossible, as we explained earlier."

Giannelli's jaw snapped shut. "It's not impossible. You just don't want to do it. Well, Mr. Ambassador, we can stand firm, too. I have tried to be polite about this. If I must be blunt, I shall. We think you owe us something for what we've done—and if Tweedlioop is as important as you say, you'll eventually come to agree. We can wait as long as you. We will deliver Tweedlioop to you as soon as we receive a goodwill gift of technical information worthy of his importance. And no sooner."

Laurie practically lunged across the table at the President. "You're using him as a *hostage!*" she exploded.

"*Shut up,*" the President said stonily, shooting her a gaze to match.

Laurie shrank back in her chair, seething silently. Danni, I noticed, didn't say a word.

And the Ambassador, with an air somehow of deep sadness, said, "No. Even Tweedlioop is not important enough for that. We will not give you what you want under any circumstances whatsoever. But we *will* take Tweedlioop home."

And with a sudden startling bound, the Ambassador left the table, a furry streak arcing between Giannelli and Goodmill to land with a soft *plop* on all fours. He scurried to the door, closely followed by his Silent Partner.

"Where are you going?" Giannelli demanded.

The Ambassador paused by the door. "To wait," he said. "But our patience is not unlimited."

Giannelli didn't try to stop them, though he hesitated visably over the decision. As soon as they were gone, he brusquely suggested that the rest of us find other ways to amuse ourselves while he conferred privately with Goodmill. We complied quietly, but Danni and I swooped down on him as soon as possible thereafter.

"*Mr.* President," Danni demanded, "what the *hell* do you think you're doing?"

He stared at her coldly, and behind the unflappable front I saw weariness and possibly fear. "I'm taking a calculated risk."

"You're using Tweedlioop as a hostage," said Danni, "just as Laurie said. Don't you remember Iran? Do you want to lower us to that level?"

"Not at all," Giannelli said wearily. "I can't tell you how much I hate to do anything that even looks that way. But as I see it, I must—and it's *not* what it looks like to you. It's a simple matter of fair play. We did something important for them. Shouldn't they do something for us?"

"Sure," I said bitterly, "and the Salvation Army should send out bills."

Danni's look reminded me to let her do the talking. "What Bill means," she said gently, "is that repayment for philanthropy is normally voluntary."

Giannelli glared first at her, then at me, exasperation plain on his face. "You're not even trying to see this my way—either of you. Can you really not see that we've earned something?"

"If we were offering a trade," said Danni, "we should have made that clear at the start. This way we're like the urchins who come up to tourists and ask to have their pictures taken and *then* demand money. Only it's worse with us. We're not urchins and we shouldn't be begging. Or playing games with a kid's life."

Giannelli shook his head. "Call it what you like. It doesn't change the facts. You must realize we're playing for very high stakes. Please—try to see it from *our* point of view for once. How much do you know of what we've learned about their space technology?"

"Not much," I said. "Nobody's told us much."

"Maybe we should have told you more. I'm sorry if we didn't handle it that well. Anyway—you know how the Ambassador arrived. We've already talked about that. We tried to examine their shuttle after they left it, but there's some kind of force field around it and we couldn't get in. But we learned some awfully interesting things from the wreck you found in Alaska; they had a lot to do with our decision to attempt contact. You saw how small that shuttle was. Didn't you wonder what kind of power plant a thing like that could have to drive it across interstellar or even interplanetary distances?"

"Sure did," I said.

"Well, it doesn't. Our Air Force men who dissected it

couldn't find anything they could recognize as a power plant. The other instrumentation is sparse and compact—even more so than we could make it with the best integrated circuits we can foresee. Yet it obviously travels, navigates, and communicates over awesome distances with uncanny precision and very high speed."

I was still frowning from a couple of sentences back. "What do you mean, no power plant? It *has* to have—"

"Not in any sense that we understand. We have a special think tank playing with some pretty wild ideas of how it works. One of the wildest is that it's a 'gravitational glider' exploiting something we don't know about the structure of space itself in a way vaguely like the way a sailplane rides thermals in the atmosphere. One of the more conservative is that a little unidentified gadget the size of a cigar box is really a power receiver and converter. The idea is that the starship that's supposedly out there has a master power plant for itself and all these little shuttles, and sends out beams—probably tachyons or something like that—which these little pink boxes convert directly into kinetic energy."

In the events of the last few weeks I'd almost forgotten I was an engineer, but ideas like those set my professional imagination racing again. What I wouldn't give for a handle on what was really behind them. . . .

"When we saw things like that," Giannelli was saying, "not in a letter from a crazy inventor but in a production-line model that obviously *worked,* we wanted it—very badly. Quite frankly, that was *our* principal goal in the decision to contact the chucks. Tweedlioop is simply not that important, in and of himself, to the American people. We couldn't justify the effort on that basis—but we *could* justify it as a means of trying to get information that would strengthen us immeasurably.

"Naturally we had to weigh the risks. We knew whoever was out there had fearsome capabilities and we weren't sure why they were here. But if they wanted to wreak havoc on us, they were already in a position to do it, and holding Tweedlioop here without acknowledging that we were doing so might well provoke it. Offering to return him, on the other hand, could only be interpreted by rational beings as a gesture of goodwill." I wondered whether he had really managed to convince himself of that. "Our hope, of course, was that their notions of ethics would be close enough to ours that they would offer some voluntary exchange. But we recognized that they might not, and that if Tweedlioop was important enough to come after at all, he would be important enough to provide bargaining leverage. The 'hostage' image problem bothered us—but after careful deliberation we decided the situation was so absolutely unique we could not be deterred by that. This is literally a once-in-history opportunity, and we simply can't pass it up. As for the threat of forceful retaliation—that is, as I said, a calculated risk. We don't think they'll do it, but we'll be watching the situation very closely. We're prepared to back down without hesitation if it becomes necessary."

He fell silent. His face was pleading for support—and I was ashamed to discover that he had almost swayed me. He was dead right about what the chucks' technology could do for us, and the temptation was strong. I wanted that capability so badly I could taste it.

But this was the wrong way to get it.

"I don't know how much you know about our space

program," the President resumed when neither Danni nor I said anything, "but—"

"I work in it," I said. "Your support for it is why I voted for you. Remember?" I knew I'd told him that, and I was quite confident he'd gotten a dossier on me when he brought me here. But I guess he'd been under enough pressure to make him forget. I doubted that I was a terribly high priority in his mind. I debated briefly and decided to try one last appeal to his conscience. "You know, Mr. Giannelli, I think you're the only politician I've ever been able to really admire. It hurts to lose that."

He ignored that, whether because it didn't register or because it cut so deeply he couldn't bear to acknowledge it. "Look," he said, "if you understand how important space is to us, how can you want to pass up even a slight chance at something like this? Especially when we've earned a perfectly legitimate claim to it. We *are* in a crisis situation, you know. Just as I told the chucks."

"I agree," I said, "and I also agree that space is a large part of the solution. But this is the wrong way to go."

There was a fleeting trace of a scowl, and then his expression hardened. "Well, I'm sorry you think so, but it's the way we are going. I've made a decision, and I'll stand by it."

Several seconds of strained silence. Then Danni asked, "So what's next, Mr. President? We don't know what they're likely to do, do we?"

"No," the President said soberly, staring at the table in front of him. "We don't know."

I was surprised at how much internal turmoil I experienced in the wake of that meeting. One thing Giannelli and I had in common was a strong, deep-seated urge to get man into space in a serious way, and soon. It wasn't just something we wanted—it was something that, after much thought, we believed was urgently necessary.

What we could learn from the chucks, if they could be persuaded to teach us, could make an enormous difference. A small part of me feared that the chuck Ambassador was right about the psychosocial side effects—that such a gift would do us more harm than good. But that was just an intellectual concession; at the levels that mattered, I wasn't at all ready to believe it. More important, I was ready to risk it. I hated the thought of their leaving without our getting any of that potential bounty, and I was prepared to do almost anything to help Giannelli get it—if I thought there was any way. I was even dismayed to find myself leaning, more than once, toward accepting his rationale for the one proposal he had.

But each time I managed to squelch it. We did *not*, I told myself sternly, have the right to extort information using Tweedlioop as a bargaining chip—even if we did not seriously intend to carry through on our threats.

For that matter, did we even have the ability—or was Giannelli playing a suicidal game? The chucks didn't seem violent, from what little we knew of them, but what if they got really mad? "Our patience is not unlimited," the Ambassador had said. . . .

What happened when it ran out?

Occasionally, among all that, I found time to wonder how Tweedlioop was doing—but not as often as I should have, and apparently I wasn't going to find out anyway. I tried—we all tried—but we could get no clue as to how he was being treated or what was happening. I hadn't forgotten, though, that he really had seemed to do best when he was with Danni and Laurie and me.

Evidently the uncertainty weighed heavily on Giannelli, too. He called late the next morning and asked Danni and me—but not Laurie—to join him for lunch. We went; the food and service were up to their usual standards, but it was quite obvious that Giannelli had something on his mind. He made a little small talk, but it wasn't long before he came to the point.

"General Goodmill and I have had quite a bit of serious discussion in the last twenty hours or so," he said. "As you well know, we can't take too lightly the possibility of some unexpected reaction against us by the chucks, and we've had to consider what kind of counter-reaction we might take. We've had to recognize that such an action might turn into a threat not only to us in this country, but to all humanity. This made us consider whether it is time to give any sort of warning to other countries. Not something we were eager to do, you'll understand. It was a delicate situation. If we lose the gamble we're taking, others need to know about the danger—and we may need their help. But if we win, we don't want to spread our gains too indiscriminately."

Danni smiled thinly. "An interesting double standard— or so it would seem to the rest of the world if word got out. Have you thought about that?"

"Of course," said Giannelli. "At great length. And the word could get out a lot easier than we'd like. If you've been following the papers, you know our preparedness moves that started as soon as this came to light have not gone unnoticed. The U.N. has been pressing for an explanation for close to three weeks, and they've been getting pretty insistent. The situation is tense. Suspicions against us are running high, and we couldn't stall much longer without giving them some sort of answer. Our intelligence gave no evidence that anyone had any inkling of the real reason for our mobilization; nor has anyone intercepted any of our transmissions to the chucks. But the kinds of guesses they'd naturally make could be more threatening to world peace than the truth—and if the truth *does* turn out to be a threat, we can't waste time trying to win back lost trust.

"So after a great deal of soul-searching, we have decided to bring the whole affair to international attention. We have told the U.N. Security Council where things stand and advised them to begin their own emergency preparations on a worldwide scale without delay. The way we told them was pretty carefully edited, of course. We still hope to work out a plan that protects everybody against a possible invasion while preserving our country's favored position if the chucks acquiesce to our wishes."

My throat felt dry. It seemed clear to me now that Giannelli *was* playing a suicidal game, unless the chucks were a lot more restrained than most humans. In a way I felt sorry for him, seeing his old idealism twisted into this kind of fanaticism. But any pity I might feel for Giannelli was dwarfed by my concern for everyone else. My political hero had become dangerous—and I didn't know how to stop him.

"Because of the obvious danger of panic," he went on, "Secretary General Dobrowski is proceeding cautiously. He will allow no word outside the Security Council until they are convinced that the danger is real and its nature properly understood. If it gets to the General Assembly, I'd guess that many details will be withheld even from them. And if it comes to a worldwide mobilization, it will probably be carried out with as little public mention as ours has been here.

"The one thing that's happening right now is a hearing in the Security Council. The Secretary General has ordered the chucks, Tweedlioop, and the human officials involved to New York for a meeting the day after tomorrow. We hope we can afford that much time; since the chucks will be included in the hearings, that seems a reasonable hope. So we go to New York tomorrow to establish temporary headquarters there—and the next morning we get down to business."

He stopped. Danni asked, "Where do we fit into all this?"

Giannelli nodded slightly. "Good question. I regret that we could not include you in the official party. The Secretary General said that was unnecessary and the hearing participants would be limited to official representatives. You're under no compulsion to have anything more to do with the case; you can go home if you like— though I need hardly remind you that the silence requirement remains absolute and will be strictly enforced. However, we appreciate your importance in bringing the whole matter to our attention and we recognize your continuing interest in Tweedlioop. So, at my suggestion, we are prepared to take you to New York and put you up in our block of rooms so you can be near the action. I can probably get you into the early hearings as spectators; you may even be able to give some testimony on our behalf. Beyond that, I can't promise much. I'm sorry

I can't offer you a more active role, but this is the best I can do."

I puzzled over his words, trying to make sure I understood what he was offering—and why. I guess Danni had got me into the habit of looking for hidden traps and devious motives, but I could see no doubt that we would want our feet as far into the door as possible.

So I was surprised to hear Danni saying, politely but firmly, and after no deliberation worth mentioning, "No, thanks, Mr. President. We'll go, but we'll arrange our own accommodations and pay our own expenses. We do appreciate your offer, of course."

I couldn't believe my ears. "Danni—" I blurted out.

And she interrupted harshly, "Not now, Bill. We'll talk about it later."

"But—"

"*Not now.* We'll talk about it later. Trust me."

I shut up, but I seethed. For the first time since I'd met her, I felt sure Danni had done something utterly wrong and irrational. I didn't know how to react to it—but I'd certainly have to find out what had gotten into her. I'd never seen her face like that—deadly serious, almost grim, with a fiercely determined set to her jaw and her lips drawn tight.

Could *I* be missing something?

Giannelli's eyebrows rose slightly at her insistence on her own odd way of doing things. "Well," he said, stroking his chin thoughtfully, "that's hardly necessary, but I suppose we can do it that way." His expression hardened slightly. "I'm sure you understand that this is a very serious matter of national and international security. A strict condition of our allowing you to go off on your own before this is all settled is that you don't leak a word about it to anyone—not even a hint. I don't mean to intimidate you, but I have to tell you that any breach of this confidence will be punished swiftly and severely. Fortunately"—a trace of smile crept back in—"we think we can trust you. That's my personal judgment, and also the official report of the psychologists who've been observing you." The smile became a slightly sheepish grin. "Sorry we couldn't tell you about them, but that would have defeated their purpose."

"Quite all right," Danni said calmly. "We're not surprised." She rose. "We're free to go?"

"Within those limits, yes. You'll need help getting out of the complex, of course. We'll fly you out to wherever you'd like to go, and then you're on your own. We'll see you in New York."

"Thank you, Mr. President. Let's go, Bill."

I followed her out of the room, still mystified by her actions. I was angry with her for the way she'd handled things, and with myself for sitting meekly by and letting her do it, and with Giannelli and his government for spying on us and for turning my simple rescue attempt into such a travesty of what I had meant it to be. But I kept all that inside until we got back to our living room.

Then I turned on Danni and let it all burst out. "What was all that about?" I demanded. I'd forgotten about Laurie, but she was locked in her room. "They're trying to buy us off, and the price isn't even very good! Are you going to just give up?"

"I don't want to talk about it now," she said curtly.

"What's gotten into you? We *have* to—"

"I said, I don't want to talk about it now. I *won't* talk

about it now." She turned away from me—but as she did so I seemed to glimpse something else behind her tough mask. A bit of hurt, I think, and something that seemed to say that she wished she *could* talk about it, but for some reason she really couldn't. But all of that was so subtle and fleeting that someone less familiar with her would have missed it entirely—and even I couldn't be sure. All I *knew* was that she was acting very different from the Danni O'Millian I had thought I knew and trusted and liked—and that hurt a lot.

"Please, Bill," she said in a softer, less confident voice. "I'll explain when we get to New York. Please trust me until then. Okay?"

I thought it over. Finally I said, "I'll try."

XI

SOMEWHAT AGAINST MY BETTER JUDGMENT, I STILL let her do the talking when we were arranging our exodus. She still couldn't find out exactly where we were, but nobody denied it was in the Appalachians at roughly Carolina or Virginia latitude. Danni told them we weren't sure whether we were going straight to New York or back to my house for a while first, so they took us to Atlanta, early the next morning.

I later found out there was never any doubt about where we were going, but she had her own reasons for not having them fly us straight to New York. They took us out on a little propjet that I didn't recognize, again flying low enough to appreciate the mountains under the crisp pre-autumn air. I'm afraid I didn't, though. I was too busy trying unsuccessfully to get a more precise fix on where we'd been—and brooding over where things stood with Danni.

I didn't entirely understand my own feelings. Theoretically, she was working for me, as my lawyer, and I thought she'd botched her job. So what? I'd often had similar clashes with people working with me or for me, but it had never bothered me like this. True, none of them had involved the fate of an interstellar crown prince being held hostage, or the threat of a war between Earth and starfaring aliens. But I didn't really think that was what was bothering me most. This, I gradually admitted to myself, was a lot more personal.

I hadn't really had much chance to see Danni as a lawyer, in any conventional sense. But I had had a lot more chance than I'd counted on to get to know her as a person—and as a person, I'd come to think of her as something pretty special. I'd tried to keep my attitudes toward her on a professional, business-relationship level—but my subconscious wasn't fooled. It had come to regard her as much more than that; and now, it seemed, she had fallen out of character.

We all sat stiffly in our seats as the plane cruised over hills and valleys, only rarely adding our voices to the drone of its engines. Sometimes I stole a sideways glance at Danni, trying to figure out which was hurting me more: my anger or my loss of faith. I couldn't decide for sure—but the worried look on her face made me worry, too. And once, incongruously, I found myself thinking that her hair still looked like spun copper and it would be worth *learning* photography to capture its sheen.

At Atlanta the plane dropped us off and taxied right back out without even shutting off its engines. We waited outside the terminal, watching it wait in line and finally take off, and then went in.

I said, "I don't suppose you're ready to tell me what's going on yet?"

"In New York," Danni repeated. "Patience, Bill. I'm not as crazy as I look."

I hoped that remark was an encouraging sign and resigned myself to following her and Laurie around the terminal. We wasted a lot of time, I thought, poking around in shops and newsstands and watching snatches of movies, but eventually we wound up at a ticket counter and Danni booked us onto a flight to New York. There were plenty of them, so we didn't have to wait long, and we were on the ground at La Guardia by noon. From there we took a taxi into Manhattan.

I'd never been in New York before, and I found the density of traffic on the expressway and the length of the trip through solid city a bit overwhelming—and not very pleasant. The aggressive New York driving added more spice than I cared for, but eventually it was over. We roared through a long tunnel lined with little white tiles and surfaced on Thirty-somethingth Street. Here there were traffic lights and stop-and-go traffic in which drivers and pedestrians seemed to be playing a perverse free-for-all game with survival as the prize. It took an absurdly long time to go each block, but we didn't have to go many. Danni had made a reservation at a hotel not far from the U.N. (I caught glimpses of that big glass box as we approached), and it was with some relief that I stepped out of the cab onto solid pavement.

The hotel looked old, with a dingy brick exterior and a Tudor lobby full of massive wooden beams. I hung back as Danni strode to the desk and said, "Reservation for Daniels?"

The clerk riffled through a file and pulled a card out. "Beulah?"

"That's right."

I frowned inwardly, but had learned to resist letting it

show. I waited while Danni finished registering under her fictitious name. I marveled again at the price, but Danni had told me that here it was considered low. The thought of what all this was costing wasn't pleasant, especially if I wound up paying it and getting nothing in the end.

A bellhop escorted us and our scant luggage to our room. Danni tipped him (lavishly, I thought) and he left, closing the door behind him. Finally, I thought, I could satisfy my curiosity. "Why the phony name?"

"Tell you later," Danni said. "I have to call somebody." She sat at the diminutive desk and dialed. I looked the place over: a pleasant enough room, in keeping with the Tudor atmosphere downstairs, but still overpriced. Actually it was two rooms: a fairly large one with two double beds and the desk and two big chairs, and a small side room with one bed.

Danni's call was answered. "Hi, Rupert," she said. "Beulah Daniels here. . . . Yes, just got in. . . . I need a room swept. . . . Right away. And can you leave a rental with me for a couple of days. . . . Great. See you soon."

She hung up. "Well, we have some time to kill. Why don't we order some lunch? And Laurie can go down to the lobby and buy some newspapers and magazines. At least a *Times* and a *New Yorker,* and whatever else strikes your fancy."

She still wouldn't say anything more profound than that. We browsed in the things Laurie bought; the three of us even laughed together over the *New Yorker* cartoons and fillers, but our laughter was forced. Another uniformed man who expected a tip brought us lunch. We were still eating when there was a knock, and Danni admitted a man in a brown three-piece suit with a thick attaché case. He opened it and took out an electronic gizmo looking vaguely like a Geiger counter. He went all over the suite, poking the gadget into nooks and crannies, as we finished eating.

And finally I had an inkling of what was going on. I relaxed a little as he finished his scan. "Looks clean," he announced finally. He put his unit away and handed another to Danni. "It's easy to use," he said. "Instructions are inside the cover."

"Thanks," she said. "I appreciate your getting here so fast."

Then he left. For the first time in too long I managed to grin at Danni. "We can talk now, right?"

She nodded. "Finally. I really appreciate your patience, Bill. I know it must have been hard."

It had; my patience had worn pretty thin. But I saw no point in rubbing that in. She knew. "You really thought they were bugging us?"

"Chances looked pretty good. We know they had psychologists watching us at Giannelli's hideout. I wasn't sure how much they'd keep spying on us after we left, but I didn't assume they'd turn us completely loose and forget about us. We know too much—and Giannelli knows we think he's wrong." She paused, looking out the window toward the U.N. building. "We can't be smug even now. I think we've managed to shake them for a while—though we can't be positive. There are some spy gadgets that can elude Rupert's detectors. We'll check the room every time we come in, but beyond that we'll have to assume we can talk here. It's the best we're going to do. Do you see now why I turned down Giannelli's offer?"

"I think so. You thought it would be safer."

"Right. I knew they'd like us to take a room of their choice—it would be like keeping us in their own private goldfish bowl. If we wanted a room that wasn't bugged, even for a little while, we'd have to get our own. This is my last chance to act a little like your lawyer and try to help you get what you want. I thought it would be worth a little extra expense and trouble to have some chance of succeeding—and Giannelli could hardly refuse without admitting *why* he wanted us to stay in their hotel."

"Understood and agreed," I said, "and apologies for being so slow to catch on." I grinned. "Who's Beulah Daniels?"

She grinned back. "I discovered a long time ago that sometimes it's handy to have an extra name that nobody knows—except a few strategically placed helpful souls like Rupert." Her expression turned serious. "Let's get down to business. Even if there's not a bug already here, it's only a matter of time, and not much of it, before there is. So this may be our only chance to talk privately. Maybe we'd better start by making sure we all understand just what everybody wants at this point. How has your view of Tweedlioop changed in view of what we've learned and what's happened?"

I considered. "Not much, really. I don't care all that much if he's an interstellar emperor-to-be. To me, he's still just a little lost kid trying to get back to his folks. What he does after that is his business."

"Hear, hear!" Laurie cheered.

"Good," said Danni. "We all agree on that. Now, what can we do about it? He's here, his folks are here with the interstellar equivalent of wheels, and all we have to do is get them together. How?"

She paused, looking at me like a teacher waiting for an answer. When I didn't give one, she started ticking off facts. "Tweedlioop wants to go home, though he has mixed feelings about it and we're not sure why. At least part of it seems to be fear of how they'll react to his failing a test.

"At the moment he's in U.S. custody awaiting international hearings to decide what to do about him. The U.S. officials are willing to return him, but only as a means to extort advanced know-how from his people. We don't know yet what the U.N. reps will want, but I'm betting their priorities will be similar: send him home, but only if they all get a slice of the technological pie. They're all afraid of war, but not necessarily enough to keep them from taking foolish risks.

"We in this room would like some of the know-how, if we can find an acceptable way to get it; but we're not willing to hold Tweedlioop for ransom. Our top priority is to get him back by whatever means necessary, with other considerations incidental. And our present power to do anything is minimal.

"Finally, the chucks agree with us that top priority is to get him back, which they insist without qualification they will do. They also insist they won't trade information. They haven't given much indication of what they'll do to get him back if the human officials won't surrender him voluntarily, but we know they *can* do an awful lot."

She stopped and I waited. It was a pretty good summary, as far as it went, but it stopped short of the key questions. "Do you think there's *any* chance," I asked, "that we can wheedle some information out of them?"

"If I did," she said soberly, "I'd be doing everything in

my power to make it happen. I want to get us out there, too. But they have us at too much of a disadvantage. They already have what we want, and I seriously doubt that we have anything they want as badly. They show no interest in Earth except as a test site for Tweedlioop, and the way I read them even he's not that crucial. If they lose him, they'll start over with a new candidate. Probably happens often enough that they routinely budget for it—and it's not likely to happen here because they *can* get him whenever they want to. The only reason they haven't already is that they're trying to be polite first. He's the only thing I see that even remotely resembles a bargaining chip for us, and he's not a very good one. I don't think it would work, and I don't think we dare risk trying it, even aside from the ethics. No, what I see is just two goals, with a distant hope of achieving one, and none at all for the other."

I sighed. "So what's going to happen?"

"That's the biggie, all right. One option is that the U.N. will decide, in what the chucks consider a reasonable time, to surrender Tweedlioop with nothing in return. Not likely on two counts. First, the U.N. doesn't do *anything* that fast. Second, they're not going to give him up for nothing unless they're scared into it.

"Option two: the chucks may back down and give them what they're asking—but I don't think so. We don't know enough about their laws or their psychology to be *sure,* but they looked pretty adamant to me. They said they're not going to give us anything, and I don't think they are. Nor do I think they're going to leave without Tweedlioop, as long as Tweedlioop is alive."

That raised a peculiarly distasteful possibility. "Do you

think any of . . . us . . . would kill him if demands aren't met?"

"No. I think they might threaten, but I don't think they'd follow through. The people in government have sense enough to realize that if they did that they couldn't expect anything good and they'd have to fear retribution. The possible nature of the retribution is too fearsome and too unknown, so the governments won't risk it—and they'll make sure he doesn't fall into the kind of hands that would. And I think all this will be obvious enough to the chucks that they'll dismiss any threat to Tweedlioop as the bluff that it is. So let's not even count that as an option."

Personally, I wasn't so sure. I hoped she wasn't assuming too much about either humans or chucks. But I resisted the urge to argue. *You brought her down as a lawyer,* a little voice told me. *Give her a chance. She can't know any less about this than you do.*

So I nodded. "Okay. What else?"

"Option three: war, but I don't think that's likely either. I don't think the chucks want any more to do with us than necessary, and I don't think they consider us a threat in the near future. Nor do I think they're very inclined to violence. Why should they put a war's worth of effort and cost and destruction into a goal that doesn't require more than a simple kidnapping?

"Hence option four: a simple kidnapping. That's the one I'm betting on. I think they'll just try to spirit him away and be done with it. Both his human guards and theirs will resist, of course, and things could get messy. Somebody could get killed, human or chuck or both. Maybe even Tweedlioop, in which case nobody wins. I don't think humans will deliberately do anything to start a war; the danger is impulsive action under pressure. But if it comes to that, I don't think the chucks will hesitate to do whatever they think is necessary. They don't need to be afraid of any countermeasures we might take if they accidentally exterminate a few of us. In the first place, they'll judge quite rightly that we'll be afraid to strike back very hard, lest they strike back even harder. And even if we do, once they've got what they want, they can just walk away and we won't be able to follow."

I sat silent for a while, looking alternately at Danni and Laurie and the overpriced room and the New York skyline. Everything she'd said was hard to consider calmly. The whole situation seemed hopeless, full of strange and unpredictable variables, and none of the likely outcomes was very appealing. Our present fix was a far cry from a month ago, when it was just Tweedlioop and me alone in the wilderness and the only question I'd faced was whether to bring him out.

And yet—I *had* foreseen, dimly, that it would lead to something like this. Now it had, and I still wasn't sure whether I'd done the right thing.

But having brought it this far, I certainly owed it to Tweedlioop to do whatever I could to push it on to our original goal.

Unfortunately, I couldn't see that there was anything I could do—and my faith in Danni's ability to do more than analyze was slipping again. "So what are we doing here?" I asked sourly. "Sounds to me like it's all out of our hands."

"If we gave up that easily," said Danni, "it would be. We start by going and listening to the U.N. I may have misjudged them, and if what I hear there lets me think it's worthwhile, I'll finagle a chance to speak to them and try to persuade them to do it our way. Meanwhile, since that doesn't look very likely and we're here on our own, we'll try to work on some alternatives."

"You really think there are any?"

"Of course—but we need freedom to work on them. As it is, they seem to think we're unimportant. I doubt that we're as free and unwatched as they let on, but we're at least better off than if they really took us seriously. So unless I see a good reason to do otherwise, I plan to keep a low profile and let them keep thinking we're unimportant as long as possible. Maybe we can accomplish something while they're not paying attention."

"Like what?"

There was a grin on Danni's face, but behind it she looked oddly serious. "Remember when I first came to Florida I said we might use extralegal methods if all else failed?"

I remembered, but . . . "I thought you were kidding."

"I wasn't. At this point the problem boils down to getting Tweedlioop together with his pickup crew. If that can't be done legally, we'll have to try something else. If the chucks try that kidnapping, maybe we can help to make sure they succeed. Maybe we'll even have to do the whole thing ourselves."

I was astonished. I'd been hoping all along that I was misjudging her with my recent doubts, but I'd had no idea my misjudgment went that far. I'd been assuming this was my problem and Tweedlioop's, and I'd felt vaguely guilty about dragging Danni into it. I appreciated her willingness to help, but I'd never expected her to take really serious risks on her own. "But, Danni," I protested, "you don't have to do that. Look, I can see that it might come to that —but if it does, let me do it. You might wind up in jail, or disbarred, or—"

"Yes," she said, her expression completely serious now, "all that might happen. And you, Bill—don't underestimate what *you're* risking."

I nodded, for the first time truly realizing that. Oddly, it didn't bother me; I had no doubt at all as to what I should do. "I started this," I said. "I should finish it. Just because I dragged you into it this far is no reason for you to throw your career away. I know how important it is to you—"

"And this is *why* it's important, Bill—to see that the decent thing is done when nobody else will do it. Don't you see that?"

I saw it and I admired it—but I didn't want her to get hurt. "But you have so much to lose. If I can do it without you—"

"And what if you can't? Look, Bill, I know you'd make a terrific effort, and you might pull it off. But even if you got him away, where would you take him? Who knows this area better, you or me?" She leaned earnestly toward me. "What does it matter who does it as long as it gets done? If we go after it together, our chances are twice as good. I know how much I'm risking, Bill. It's worth it. If you want me out because you don't want me along anymore, I'll leave. But if you're just trying to protect me, forget it. I don't need it. I'm in as deep as you are and I want us to see it through to the end. Together." She leaned back and looked at me. "So am I in or am I out?"

I thought about it for a long time, but there was only one thing I could say. "You're in, Danni. And am I glad."

I felt a sudden urge to hug her, but somehow I didn't think I deserved it just then. So I gave myself a rain check and hoped that someday I could ask her to honor it.

Later that afternoon we walked by a circuitous route to the hotel where Giannelli's party was staying. It was far more modern than ours, a tall, boxy tower of tinted glass on a steel frame, a little reminiscent of the U.N. itself and only a stone's throw away. Giannelli and his entourage had taken the whole top floor, and security was very tight. There were guards surrounding the elevator doors— dressed in conservative business suits, but obviously guards nonetheless—and they converged on us as soon as we stepped out, even though we'd called ahead from the lobby. They demanded proofs of identity and frisked all of us—even Laurie—before two of them escorted us down a long hallway to a suite whose door was flanked by still more guards.

Inside was a spacious vestibule decorated with potted palms. The sole furnishing was a starkly modern desk behind which sat the same receptionist who had first admitted us to Giannelli's presence. She recognized us and smiled. "Hello, Ms. O'Millian, Mr. Nordstrom. Did you have a pleasant trip?"

"Pleasant enough," said Danni. "Has the President arrived?"

"Yes, he has. May I help you?"

"We wanted to let Mr. Giannelli know we're here. We'd also like to see Tweedlioop."

The receptionist pursed her lips. "I'm afraid I can't authorize that." As she talked, she punched buttons on her intercom. "I don't know when the President will be able to see you. Would you like to leave your names and where you're staying? I'm sure he'd like to have your phone number in any case."

"That won't be necessary," said Danni. "We probably won't be there much anyway. But we'll be checking back here several times a day. We'd appreciate it if you'd tell him we stopped by." She turned toward the door.

And another door opened at the side of the vestibule. "Ah," said Giannelli, "what fortunate timing. I almost missed you." He came forward, greeting us with smiles and handshakes. Through the door behind him I saw the sprawling panorama of city through a huge plate-glass window. "Awfully glad you came by. I hope you'll be pleased with the way things come out. If there's anything you need, don't hesitate to call."

Even I knew better than to take that at face value. But Danni played the game with her pleasantest manner. "That's very kind of you, Mr. President. We'll try not to impose, but we appreciate the offer. As a matter of fact, there is one little thing. It's been a couple of days since we've seen Tweedlioop, and I suspect the events of those days have been as traumatic for him as for us. We'd feel a lot better if we could visit him and see how he's doing."

"I understand," said Giannelli, "and I'm really sorry I can't oblige you the way I'd like to. But I'm afraid we can't admit *anyone* to see him at this point—not even the Ambassador. You understand we have to be very careful in a security matter as unprecedented and delicate as this." He let his expression brighten just a little. "But I do appreciate your concern for him, and I recognize that your interest is special. Maybe we can bend the rules just a little. I can assure you that both he and the Ambassador's party are being kept quite comfortable. But no doubt you'd like to see for yourselves. Tell you what. I'll personally show you the Ambassador's quarters, and I'll arrange for someone to show you Tweedlioop's. Will that do?"

"Well," said Danni, "it's not quite what we'd hoped for, but we'll appreciate whatever you can do."

It seemed to me that she ought to be trying harder to get what we really wanted: a chance to talk to Tweedlioop. But I didn't say anything. I was learning.

Giannelli, unobtrusively accompanied by two of the ubiquitous Secret Service men, led us through a maze of long halls to a suite much like his. The guards were even thicker here, and the ones inside the vestibule made no pretense of concealing their function. They were *Soldiers*, and the paraphernalia they wore was clearly intended to keep that fact uppermost in the mind of anyone seeing them. It worked on me; I would not have cared to tangle with one of those submachine guns.

They all saluted smartly, and Giannelli returned their salutes. "At ease, gentlemen. This is Mr. Nordstrom, who found the first alien, and his attorney. They'd like to see our visitors' quarters."

"Yes, sir," said the guard with the most stripes. "Shall we let them inside?"

"That won't be necessary, Sergeant. The window will be sufficient."

"Yes, sir." The senior sergeant pressed a button, and a picture on the wall split neatly down the middle. The halves slid silently back, revealing a foot-square pane of clear glass through which we could see the suite's parlor.

"One-way glass," Giannelli explained. "As you can see, they're quite comfortable."

It was only later that I thought much about the ethics of spying on visiting diplomats through one-way glass. It's probably just as well. The Ambassador and the Silent Partner did look reasonably comfortable, to my untrained eye. They looked very small in the big room. All the standard furniture was still there, but some of it had been pushed aside and supplemented by much smaller pieces of completely unfamiliar design. The two honorable chucks faced each other across a tiny table, alternately talking to each other and partaking of food and drinks from the table. "They have an advantage," Giannelli said, "in being able to talk to us in English. We asked them what they'd like to make their stay comfortable, they told us, and we made it. They also made some suggestions for Tweedlioop, and he's quite comfy too. Well . . . Satisfied?"

"I suppose so," Danni said. "Thank you, Mr. President." Giannelli nodded to the sergeant, who pressed the button to reassemble the picture. Just before the room vanished, I noticed the exterior window on the far side. It was as big as the President's, and thinly covered by a sheer curtain—but that couldn't hide how it was fitted with a heavy metal grate, with no openings big enough for a chuck.

Giannelli took us back to his suite and turned us over to one of the excess Secret Service men. "Mr. Johnson will take you to see Tweedlioop's lodgings. Thanks for coming by. I'll see you at the hearings tomorrow morning."

Tweedlioop was in a different hotel some blocks away —ironically, closer to ours. Johnson took us there in a black car he called up from the hotel garage. Tweedlioop occupied the penthouse, as heavily guarded and refurnished in much the same way as the Ambassador's suite, even to the heavily grated window. We saw it through the same kind of one-way peephole. He was reclining on one of the custom furnishings, staring out the window, and Laurie blurted out, "Can't we go in? Just for a minute?"

"I'm sorry," our escort said stiffly, "I have my orders."

Laurie tried to persuade him, but to no avail. Meanwhile, Tweedlioop's head jerked around as if looking at us. But he didn't seem to see, and I guessed that he'd heard and recognized our voices. For an instant he seemed to start toward the door, then stopped as if thinking better of it. But he did chatter; I heard him faintly through the door. . . .

"Time to go," said Johnson, closing the window. "You've seen he's safe."

Laurie was half crying, and Danni literally had to pull her away. "Good-bye, Tweedlioop!" Laurie called after her. "We'll come back to see you somehow. We'll get to talk again. . . ."

Eventually Danni got her quieted down, but not until our elevator was halfway to street level. Johnson offered us a ride to our hotel; Danni politely but firmly declined.

He went on to the garage, and we walked briskly in the other direction. A minute or so later we were pretty sure we saw his car drive off, but Danni was still wary. She took us for a walk, pointing out sights as we passed, saying not a word about anything we'd just been shown. We went into Grand Central Terminal and merged into rush-hour crowds that reminded me of gas molecules darting madly hither and yon and occasionally bouncing off one another. Danni pointed out the Kodak Colorama, the huge back-lighted transparency at one end of the hall. This month, interestingly, it featured a view of Denali, not far from where I'd met Tweedlioop, and that stirred up all kinds of associations. I stared, fascinated, but we never stopped moving and Danni never quit watching the people swarming around us.

Finally she said, "I think we're okay, now. Everybody know the way back to the hotel?" Laurie and I nodded. "Good. Let's go back separately. Don't go too straight, but let's meet there in twenty minutes."

And she was off. In mere seconds she had vanished into the crowds. Laurie and I followed her example.

I had less trouble than I expected finding my way back. Fortunately, midtown Manhattan's layout is pretty straightforward.

But I was the last to get back. I think we were all relieved when I walked in and saw them in the lobby, and even more so when we locked ourselves into our room. Danni went over the place with her rented scanner, looking for any bugs that had been added since we left.

Then she said wryly, "Well, we can still hope they don't know where we're staying. We can even hope they don't care—but we can't count on it." She settled into one of the chairs. Laurie took the other, and I stretched out on one of the beds.

"So how does it look?" I asked.

"Well, the good news is that Giannelli's patronizing us. He made a big show of coming out to see us and show us the Ambassador's place because he wants us to think they think we're important. But they don't, really."

"How do you know?"

"If they did, this place would be bugged. My guess is that they think if they make us feel important, we'll stay happy enough to refrain from doing anything really pesky. They underestimate us." She paused. "Mind you, we mustn't underestimate them. They don't seem to be watching us as closely as they might, but I don't believe for a minute they're really ignoring us. If nothing else, they could have followed one of us back here, and I'd be surprised if they didn't. We have to assume that our little visit cost us any faint hope of real secrecy we might still have."

I closed my eyes, having studied the ceiling enough for a while. "And you still think we can do anything really pesky? Those prisons they have there . . ."

"Well, that does bring us to the bad news, but I'm not ready to give up. The bad news is that with all the guards and special locks and window grates and such, I don't see much chance of the Ambassador and his friend getting out of theirs or into Tweedlioop's. So if it's up to them, that kidnapping I predicted isn't likely to come off. And our chances aren't much better. Unless there are more chucks somewhere, and they have capabilities we don't know about, nobody's going to spirit Tweedlioop away."

"So what do we do?"

"We keep looking for something we've overlooked. Meanwhile, we pay real close attention to those hearings tomorrow. Reasoning with the Security Council may be our only hope."

We didn't talk much the rest of the evening. I think we were all too busy thinking, and afraid to say anything lest the others confirm our fears. We ate supper together but in relative silence, and when my first night in New York fell, we all went early to such sleep as we could manage —Danni in one of the beds in the main room, I in the other, and Laurie in the extra room.

The U.N. hearings started at nine, so we had the desk clerk call us at eight. We walked over; it was a crisp, clear morning, and the skyscrapers gleamed under a sky of deep blue such as I had never associated with New York. But Danni assured me they happened oftener than I might think.

"But it is nice," she added. "Nippy, too. I think fall's coming on. Did you pack some warm clothes?"

"A few," I said. "Layering gets pretty deeply ingrained in backpackers."

"Good. If you hadn't, we might have to take the afternoon off and go shopping for you."

I wasn't sure how to take that. Was she mothering me —or teasing me by pretending to? Or did she have more plans in the works than she'd told me about?

Maybe so. She hadn't slept much better than I had.

We had to show identification, and a uniformed guard had to verify us with somebody else by telephone before we could get near the Security Council chamber. We were checked at the door for cameras and recording equipment; recording, we were told, would be restricted to a single officially made and heavily guarded videotape.

The chamber struck me as unnecessarily big and lavish for a dozen and a half people to sit and talk, but that didn't really surprise me. There was a spectators' gallery at the back, behind a glass partition, but we were the only people in it. The proceedings didn't start quite on time, so I had a little time to study the layout while the delegates filed in, milled around, and took their places. Long center table, almost surrounded by a circular one; plush-draped walls and murals and carefully arrayed flags. . . . There was a microphone in front of each delegate's chair, and Danni showed me how to use the earphone attached to my chair and dial up a running translation of the proceedings in any of a dozen languages.

A bald man I recognized as Secretary General Jan Dobrowski took his seat on a dais with a commanding view of the whole assembly. Giannelli was seated beside and slightly behind him, facing the other delegates.

Dobrowski rapped for order and got it. I tensed up a little, because I knew and cared about what was being decided. But it took a surprising amount of effort to stay awake, much less tense. As Danni had hinted, everything that happened took place slowly and ponderously. Things of substance were said, but their real import was carefully packaged in layers of circumlocution. With difficulty, I resisted the urge to fidget through the whole first session; Laurie could not.

Dobrowski started things off with an eloquent speech filling the delegates in on the general situation. I suspected they had already been briefed, but he didn't let himself be hurried or take anything for granted. Quite early and frequently thereafter, like the recurring theme of a rondo, he stressed the need for absolute secrecy outside this room. He stated the basic facts as he had been told them: that technologically sophisticated aliens had come to our solar system, that they might or might not pose a threat, but that they surely offered an unprecedented opportunity to gain knowledge and wisdom that might take us centuries or millenniums to develop on our own. He told of the U.S. role so far, and here his words were double-edged, with both edges guarded by a translucent scabbard of diplomatic phraseology. He did not mention me or Danni by name; he said only that a crashed shuttle had been found on American soil and a single survivor was in American custody. The Americans, he said, had contacted others, from whom they had learned that the survivor was very young but very important—remotely comparable to a crown prince in a human monarchy. Recognizing both the crown prince's negotiating potential and the dangers of misjudging how to use it, the American President had brought the matter to the Security Council for cooperative action. With one edge Dobrowski praised Giannelli for not continuing unilaterally with actions that could have worldwide repercussions; with the other he condemned him for waiting so long. But he did not dwell on that. Even during a reprimand, the mutual, ritual respect of statesmen must be preserved.

"Mr. Giannelli's hope," Dobrowski intoned, "is that we will be able to persuade our extraterrestrial visitors that our care and return of their crown prince should be rewarded by some sharing of knowledge. But hand in hand with that hope goes the fear that our efforts at rational persuasion will be misconstrued and lead to violent action against Earth which we may be ill prepared to withstand. For that reason, the first action recommended by Mr. Giannelli is a military mobilization by U.N. forces and all our member nations—not for use against one another, but for defense against a common foe.

"I cannot emphasize too strongly that we do not yet know that the visitors *are* a foe. We hope that they are not —but we must be prepared for the worst possibility.

"I realize that this whole situation is so far out of our past experience that before you can recommend concrete action you must be quite sure that the situation is in fact as I have described it. To that end I have asked President Giannelli to speak to us today. He has promised us proof so undeniable that we could put doubt from our minds and get down to business. Ladies and gentlemen, the President of the United States."

Brief, scattered applause as Giannelli rose to the lectern. He spoke as formally as Dobrowski, and with as many layers of veiled meaning. He did not speak long. Most of what he might have said, Dobrowski had already covered—largely from Giannelli's script. Giannelli spoke magnanimously of hope that mankind could act in concert to achieve results that would benefit all—but he hinted, between the lines, that the U.S. had already established a position of leadership in dealing with the aliens and expected a proportionate share of the rewards.

"But I sincerely believe," he concluded, "that if this unparalleled opportunity is handled properly by this august body, it should be richly rewarding to everyone—not only to us on Earth, but to our visitors themselves. And what more appropriate way to begin our work toward that goal than by introducing our Ambassador from the stars?"

At the cue, a side door opened and a guard admitted the Ambassador and his Silent Partner. They ran across the floor, unseen by half the delegates, and scurried as if effortlessly up onto the long central table. I couldn't see how they gripped it, but they *were* quite light. . . .

There were a few stifled gasps from delegates at first sight of the chucks, but for the most part they took it in stride. The Ambassador gave a brief and empty greeting; I speculated that they must have evolved diplomatic protocols not too unlike ours, but had finally trimmed some of the fat out. Within minutes, delegates were making little welcoming speeches, simultaneously extending metaphorical open arms and hinting that this shouldn't have happened without overt consent. There followed a question-and-answer period in which the representatives of *Homo sapiens* tried to feel out whom they were dealing with. Some of it was embarrassingly like a TV quiz show or putting a pet through paces, but the Ambassador's composure never slipped. He quickly established himself as a genuinely intelligent and highly principled being, at least the equal of anyone else in the room.

At quarter of eleven, Dobrowski suggested a break and asked the Ambassador if he could summarize in a few words what his government was asking and what they were prepared to offer in return. "It is very simple," said the Ambassador. "We ask the return of Tweedlioop. We offer our gratitude for a deed of common decency, and we promise to leave your system immediately and not return. I regret that we can offer nothing else."

"Not even," said Dobrowski, "a modicum of technological information?"

"Not even that," said the Ambassador. "I have explained this at some length to Mr. Giannelli."

"And if we refuse to return Tweedlioop without such an exchange?"

"We will not leave without him," said the Ambassador.

"Thank you, Your Excellency." Dobrowski's voice was meticulously expressionless. "We will now take a fifteen-minute recess."

The assembly of diplomats exploded into a hubbub of animated two- and three-way conversations. Danni said, "Let's go out for a drink," and we adjourned to the nearest section of corridor, sealed off from the building at large and empty except for us. There was a drinking fountain there, and a pair of restrooms, and a phone booth. As I was getting a drink, Laurie said, "Mommy, what's going on in there? What are they going to do to Tweedlioop? Is there going to be a war?"

"I wish I knew," Danni told her. "We'll talk about it

later. I have to make some phone calls." She went into the phone booth and stayed there for most of the recess.

When she came out and we started back to our seats, I asked her, "Danni, what *is* going on in there?"

"Talk," she said. "As for what's going to happen, it's too early to say. We may know more in an hour or two."

When the Council reconvened, the chucks were conspicuously gone. Giannelli was still there, and he'd had the Ambassador's shuttle brought in as an exhibit. How had he done that, someone asked. Simply enough: the chucks had refused to come unless it came with them. They'd insisted on riding inside it as it was carried by jet and truck, though they hadn't objected to leaving it once they were here. Giannelli told what was known about it, and the assembled delegates were duly impressed and covetous.

And then the fur began to fly. With the Ambassador out of earshot and the prize palpably present, the delegates began to debate possible actions. On one they agreed quite easily: immediate worldwide mobilization. On one other they came close: the determination to hold Tweedlioop as a hostage to pry technological secrets out of the chucks. On details there was chaos. Dobrowski had his hands full controlling heated exchanges about how any knowledge gained was to be shared, how the Council's demands for such knowledge could be backed up, and how far they would be pushed before they were considered intolerably dangerous. Wilbur Giannelli caught flak from all quarters for having kept the secret this long and for his apparent determination to keep a lion's share of anything that was gained for the U.S.

From the start, two themes were dominant. One was the

fierce determination to get *something* for Tweedlioop's return—with each delegate wanting as much as possible for his own country, for each considered his needs more desperate than anyone else's. The other was a disquieting brashness in regard to the military threat. "We will back down when necessary," each delegate seemed to say, "and no sooner."

But no one offered a clear criterion for recognizing necessity when it arose.

Both themes grew steadily louder and more insistent as the session pounded on; and by one o'clock, when Dobrowski declared a long-overdue lunch break, I didn't feel much like eating.

Danni looked grim as we left the Council chamber. "Doesn't look good," she muttered. "I don't think I'd gain a thing by talking to that bunch." She ducked into the phone booth and stayed on the phone quite a while with a single call. When she came out she was smiling slightly.

I frowned. "What was all that about?"

"I made us a dinner appointment for tonight," she said. "I want you to meet an old friend of mine."

"Doesn't that seem a bit . . . uh . . . *frivolous* at a time like this?"

"You should never get too busy for old friends," she said earnestly—and then she winked. "You never know when they'll come in handy. Come on, let's get something to eat. We need a break—and we'll need another one by tonight."

She was right. The afternoon sessions were, if possible, even less encouraging, and by five o'clock I was feeling pretty low. "Relax, Bill," Danni told me as we left the building. "Worrying won't help, and it's not good for you."

I agreed, in principle. But she didn't look all that cheerful, either.

We went back to Grand Central, this time without dodging maneuvers, and caught a Lexington Avenue subway uptown. It was an experience: both station and train were dirty and noisy and crowded and harshly lit, and the car was jerky and *covered* with graffiti. We had to stand up and hang on, but at least it was fast. In just a few minutes we got off at Eighty-sixth Street and were back out in the open.

It was a relatively refreshing neighborhood—mostly residential, the streets lined with rows of picturesque old apartment buildings, and with a good deal less traffic and bustle than the Grand Central area. In odd moments I'd been learning how New York was laid out, but here I just followed Danni's lead. She made several turns, pointing out sights. "This is where I lived," she said, smiling as she gestured at a four-story brownstone with a plain stoop leading to an elaborately carved front door. There were multiple locks on the door and iron bars over the first-floor windows. "We were on the third floor, by the gargoyles. I used to lean out the windows and hang tinsel on them at Christmas." She laughed and turned toward the end of the street, where late sunlight squeezed through a green wall of trees. "That's Central Park. Remember? My introduction to greenery."

I found my attention oddly absorbed. It intrigued me to think that this was where Danni had grown up, and try to picture her as a little girl here and imagine how that had helped shape her into the person she was now. We were walking again, and soon I followed her up the stairs of another house, fairly similar in style. The front door was unlocked and we went right in, but another door inside the tiny vestibule sported even more locks than the one on Danni's old building. She studied the mailboxes that covered one wall, selected one labeled "L. Sendelman," and pressed a white button next to the nameplate.

"Yes?" said a woman's voice distorted by a cheap intercom.

"Hi, Lois. It's Danni O'Millian."

"Danni!" the speaker squealed. "Come right up." At the sound of a buzzer, Danni opened the inner door to let us through.

The hall beyond was dingy, and fragrant with age and a dozen kinds of cooking. There was a small elevator, but we climbed the stairs and Danni said we'd probably get there faster.

The door marked 4B had another buzzer, three locks visible from the hall, and a peephole. But we passed inspection, and the door flew open on a beaming young woman who greeted Danni with an effusive hug. "It was such a nice surprise to hear from you!" she exclaimed. "When you went off to Alaska, I was afraid I'd seen the last of you. Are you back to stay?"

"Oh, no," said Danni, "just here on business. I'm working on a case. I'd like you to meet my client and good friend, Bill Nordstrom. Bill, this is Lois Sendelman. We both grew up here and went to school together."

"I'm *so* glad to meet you, Bill," Lois gushed. I assured her I was glad to meet her, too, and then faded back as she marveled at how Laurie had grown. My first impression was that Lois Sendelman didn't seem like Danni's kind of people, and I wondered why Danni had been so anxious to come and see her. She was about Danni's age, I guessed, but somehow looked older. She was slim and sleekly groomed, with subtly waved gold-blond hair and fashionably expensive clothes, but her face depended heavily on makeup that seemed to me an overdone effort to appear underdone. So did her manner.

But Danni called her an old friend, and I took that as high recommendation. So I tried to reserve judgment.

"My goodness," Lois was saying, "I'm not a very good hostess, am I? It's the excitement of seeing you again, I guess. Here, you sit down and make yourselves comfortable and I'll get you some drinks. . . ."

Danni and I said white wine would be fine, and Laurie ordered cream soda. We waited on a long white sofa while Lois went to get them. The room was a little too formal and museumlike for my tastes, but nicely done and well kept. It certainly made a dazzling contrast to the drab hallways. And aromas hung in the air that bespoke an excellent meal to come.

Lois came back in a few minutes and passed out drinks in crystal glasses from an engraved silver tray. "I brought a few *hors d'oeuvres,*" she said as she set the tray down on a glass coffee table. "Help yourselves." She sat down in an upholstered chair and lifted her glass. "To old friends!"

We echoed the toast and settled back to sipping, munching, and small talk. "I hope I'm not treading on sensitive ground," Lois said carefully, to Danni, "but you haven't mentioned Jim. Are you two . . . still together?"

"We were," said Danni. "Jim died in an accident three years ago. We were together when it happened."

"Oh. I'm sorry." The inevitable awkward pause. A look

of wistful sadness came over Lois's face. "I hope you won't take this the wrong way, but maybe you were lucky, in a way. For two years I was living with a guy I met at the agency. I honestly thought he was the answer to all my dreams, and it just kept getting better and better. . . . And then he just walked out on me. Like that!" She snapped her fingers and stared into her glass. "I still see him on the streets once in a while—but I try not to." She took a long swallow, and I felt like an intruder. "I think the way it happened with you and Jim was better."

"Yes," Danni said softly, "I think it was. I'm sorry, Lois. But you'll bounce back." She eased away from the subject. "Are you still modeling?"

"No. I . . . got out of that. I've been working for a publisher, but I'm not sure I want to stay with that. I've been thinking about interior decorating."

"Good idea. You've certainly done a nice job here."

Lois's grief dissolved into a smile of childlike pleasure. "You really like it? Thank you." She laughed self-consciously. "I'd hoped to be out of this place by now. Too many memories. But the way rents are these days, and it's so hard even to find a decent place. . . ." She shrugged. "Redecorating helps."

"I think it looks terrific," Danni repeated. "How about your car? Do you still have that?"

"The Mercedes? Yes. Still runs fine, too, but I seem to drive it less and less. A car's such a bother in the city, and you have to drive so far to get out where it isn't. Mostly it just sits in Todd's Garage running up bills. Sometimes I wonder whether it's worthwhile. Maybe I ought to get rid of it."

"Hm-m-m," Danni mused, "maybe I should buy it. I

could take it home up the Alcan. . . . You know, now that I mention it, maybe I will test-drive it, if you don't mind. Might even be able to fit that into the line of duty. We may have to make a little run out to Connecticut sometime while we're here, and we may be in a bit of a hurry. Any chance I could borrow the car if you're not using it? I know it's a big favor to ask, but I'll leave it with a full tank."

"No problem at all," said Lois. "Glad to help out. Just say the word." She glanced at me and then back at Danni. "Trouble?"

"Oh, no," Danni said lightly. "Just business. But you know how fast deals can come and go."

"Yes. Well, you can count on me." She looked at her watch. "Dinner should be about ready. I hope you brought your appetites."

We adjourned to the dining room and ate. Lois was a good cook, and she'd pulled out all the stops. The menu was French, from *escargots* to *coq au vin* to some exquisite light pastries, and I couldn't remember having better. But the conversation stayed in the same vein, and Lois made little effort to include Laurie or me in it. I never felt really comfortable, and I passed the evening largely wondering what was happening with Tweedlioop and what Danni had been talking about when she asked Lois about borrowing her car to go to Connecticut. I was relieved when Danni finally told Lois we had an early appointment (to her credit, Lois never asked just what our New York business was), and we had to leave.

It was quite late by then, and the subway was a lot less crowded—which made its noise seem all the louder. I was a little glad to see a uniformed policeman aboard our car.

We didn't talk much during the brief ride, but at one point I did think I'd figured out one of my answers. I leaned close to Danni and asked, "Did Lois's car have much to do with our visit tonight?"

She nodded but didn't speak.

"Connecticut?" I asked.

"Maybe not Connecticut." I could tell her spirits were below par. "Probably not Connecticut. I just wanted to see if we had wheels if we got a sudden hankering to go somewhere. Trouble is, right now I don't have any idea where we'd go—or how we'd get anybody to go with us."

Her words were veiled, but I knew what she meant—and I realized with sudden surprise that she was fighting back tears. After we got off the train and were walking along semi-deserted streets to our hotel—this time by the shortest route—we found ourselves holding hands. I don't know who started it.

We went to bed as soon as we got back, and Danni rechecked for bugs. Laurie closed the door to her room, and Danni and I got into our beds and shut off the lights.

I don't think either of us got very close to sleep. After we'd been lying there in the darkness for a while, I heard Danni's voice, sounding oddly small, say, "Bill?"

"Yes?"

"Do you prefer sleeping over there by yourself?"

As I've said before, sometimes I'm not too astute. Her question caught me by surprise. "What do you mean?"

"Well, I don't know about you, but the way I feel right now—I sure could use being held."

"So could I." A moment later I was slipping into her bed and we were both being held quite snugly. It was the first time I'd been that close to anybody since before the fire, and I was shocked to discover that I'd forgotten how good it can feel. But it didn't take long to learn again. Briefly, for the first time in weeks, I thought of Kit, and somehow I felt that she was as happy for me as I was for myself.

Danni and I both felt a whole lot better as we lay there some time later, her warm arms draped across me and mine across her, sinking slowly toward sleep. We must have gotten pretty close, because it took quite a while before either of us really noticed the scratching on our door. (You know how it is when you wake to a ringing telephone?)

But eventually it registered enough for Danni to murmur, "What's that, Bill?"

"I dunno. Dog, maybe?"

"What's he doing here? And why does he keep scratching on *our* door?"

I groped for an answer. Something was prickling at the back of my mind, but before I recognized it the scratching stopped, just for a second or two.

And that brief pause was filled by a faint—but unmistakable—fluting sound.

"Tweedlioop!" Danni shrieked, and before the word was out she had bolted out of bed and pulled her robe more or less on and turned on a light and opened the door.

By the time I got there, still pulling my robe around me and forcing the realization into my skull, the outside door was closed again. Danni was leaning against it and shaking.

And in her arms, clutched tightly against her and shaking just as much but faster, was a familiar little ball of fluff named Tweedlioop.

210

XII

THE ONE THING WE'D FORGOTTEN WAS THAT
Tweedlioop himself was not a passive object, but a living
individual with initiative and capabilities of his own. It
had been easy to forget that, with first his sickness and
depression and limited communication and later his apparent decision to trust us to help him. Now, it seemed,
he had realized how little we could do, and somehow he'd
managed something on his own.

But the job wasn't finished. I'd recognized his one brief
utterance outside the door. It was the one phrase of his
language I knew—the one I'd distorted into our name for
him.

The one Laurie said meant, "I need help."

I stroked his head and talked softly to him, but I didn't
expect him to understand. Laurie had said he had trouble
hearing my low frequencies; I wondered how many of his
highs I missed.

Laurie's door opened and she emerged in her long flowered nightgown. She still looked half asleep. "What's all
the fuss out here? I'm trying to—" And then she saw
Tweedlioop. Her eyes sprang wide open and she ran over

211

to Danni and cradled his face in her hands. "Tweedlioop! How did you get out? How did you find us?"

He rubbed his cheek against her hand and twittered. "Really?"

"What's he saying?" Danni asked.

"He says he knew we were nearby because he heard us and smelled us when we visited where they were keeping him. But . . ." She stopped to listen as he chattered some more. "He knew we couldn't get in to him, with all the guards and locks and everything, and he knew time was running out. So he decided he'd better try to take things into his own hands. He says, 'I should have done it earlier. I *am* supposed to be Ruler stock, after all!' " She giggled. "But how—"

He answered torrentially before she finished the question. She missed some of it and asked for several clarifications, using unintelligibly terse English phrases interspersed with chirps. Finally she told us, "At first he thought there was no way he could get out, but apparently his jailers didn't think hard enough about what his size might mean. His room had air vents with grills over them. He couldn't take the grills off, but each one had a small movable section that he could squeeze past. Then he could feel his way through the dark air shafts through the building. Finally he came out in another room and hid there until somebody opened a door so he could sneak out. Then he wandered through the building and picked up our scent and followed it here." She shivered. "That must have been a scary trip. You're brave, Tweedlioop."

I was impressed. "But why here?" I asked. "Why us? Why didn't he go straight to the Ambassador?"

Laurie relayed my question to Tweedlioop and translated his answer back to us. "What good would it do?" he asked. "I had no scent trail to follow, since they were in a different building and had never been to mine. Even if I had, I doubt I could have got past their guards. And even if I did that, how would we get back out? If their ventilators were like mine, they couldn't get into them. They're too big. It was easier to come here, and if I could get this far, you could help me do the rest. Maybe you can get them out, somehow, and get us together. . . ."

He looked up at me hopefully. My mind was racing. What he'd done so far was nothing less than heroic—but if it was to pay off, he was back to trusting us. This was my last chance to finish what I'd set out to do when I went back down the canyon to save him from the wolves. I was overwhelmed by his trust—and my inability to think of anything to do to deserve it.

And then, in a sudden flash of inspiration, I did—at least partly. "If we could take him off to some place hard to find," I said, "and get a secret message to the Ambassador and trick the guards into letting him out and back to the shuttle, so he could come and meet us—"

"But how will we do all that?" said Danni. "Sure, we can use Lois's car to go somewhere. . . . Hm-m-m, I even have an idea where. But how do we get a message to the Ambassador?" She glanced at the clock radio on the stand between the beds and scowled. "We'd better figure something out soon. They've probably already noticed he's missing, and they'll be searching. The sooner we get well away from here, the better." She chewed her lip in frustration. "We obviously can't *take* a message to the Ambassador. . . ."

Suddenly Laurie said, "Tweedlioop, can you write?"

He didn't understand at first, but she carried him to the desk and got a pen and some hotel stationery from the top drawer. "Remember when I read you the comics? Marks on paper that mean words. See? Like this." She wrote something and read it back, pointing at each word as she said it. "We . . . want . . . to . . . help . . . you . . . go . . . home." She offered him the pen. "Can you do that—in your language?"

He took the pen, awkwardly. He looked like a kindergartner with one of those grotesquely oversized pencils they're subjected to, only more so. He could barely handle it, and even I could tell that the marks he made were pretty shaky.

But they certainly looked like a very foreign writing system, and when he'd finished, he pointed at successive symbols and chirped at each one. "See?" Laurie beamed. "He wrote the same thing I did. He can write a message for the Ambassador that nobody else can read—"

"And we can leave it right here," I finished excitedly. "And head out to Danni's rendezvous point. And when we're almost there, we can call Giannelli's people and tell them to look here."

"We may not even have to call," Danni said grimly. "But however they get it, they'll have to take it to the Ambassador and turn him loose to go after Tweedlioop—because it's their only clue to his whereabouts and the chucks certainly won't tell them what it says. They'll be racing to get there first, with Giannelli's people following the chucks, and if the humans get there first we're back where we started. But if the chucks win, they can probably get away, with Tweedlioop. Okay, Bill—good plan. Not perfect, but we don't have time to hold out for a better one. Let's get down to business."

Tweedlioop said something. "He wants to know what to write," Laurie explained.

"Tell them you're safe and ready to go home," Danni said, speaking directly to Tweedlioop and trusting Laurie to clarify as needed. "Tell them to look for us at . . . Hm-m-m, the name won't help anyway, and I'd better whisper the description, in case we're more bugged than I thought." We all leaned close to Tweedlioop. Laurie had to amplify pretty often, and Tweedlioop had trouble writing with the human-sized pen, so it took quite a few minutes to get through the short note. "Follow the Hudson River—the big one going north from the city—about 35 miles. There a range of low mountains, roughly 1000 to 1500 feet high, crosses the river from southwest to northeast, and the river narrows. Follow the river another nine or ten miles, watching the mountains on the west side, right along the river. We'll be on the last one; after that there's a big, wide valley. The summit is wooded. Look for us on the open, rocky slope between there and the cliff top on the southeast side. We should be there by dawn." Pause. "Okay, Tweedlioop. That's it. Let's grab what we must and hit the road."

She took the paper and wrote "TO THE AMBASSA-DOR" prominently at the top. Then she tucked it under the ashtray on the desk, just enough to hold but not hide it, and we all scurried briskly about the room. We dressed hurriedly. At Danni's insistence we grabbed every sweater and jacket we had, and she yanked the blanket off our bed. Together we folded it, and then she went to the phone and dialed.

She let it ring a long time, and I could hear that the

voice that finally answered was disgruntled even though I couldn't recognize many words. "Hi, Lois," Danni said, projecting urgency from her very first word. "Sorry to call you at this hour, but something's come up. I had no idea it would be this soon. . . . No, it can't wait. . . . Later, sure. No time now. But if I can use your car—As soon as a cab can get us there. We're leaving now."

She stopped and Lois waited several seconds. Then I understood, "You *are* in trouble, aren't you, Danni?"

"You might say that. I can't explain now, but I'll try later. I really need your help, Lois. Right now. . . . Great. Thanks a lot. See you in a jiffy."

She hung up. "Okay, folks. This is it. Bill, you'd better carry Tweedlioop in your coat." As I tucked him in, she came over and whispered to him, "And please be quiet, little fella. We don't want anybody to know you're there."

Then we left, locking the door but leaving the lights on.

It was quite nippy outside, and traffic was sparse. We waited several minutes before we even saw a taxi, and when we did we couldn't take it because Danni saw something else. "That fellow up the block on the other side," she whispered, "has been watching us almost since we got here. And now he's edging this way."

I remembered stories, and something caught in my throat. "Mugger?"

"Maybe worse." She waved the cab on. "Bill, you turn inconspicuously away from him and let Tweedlioop out of your coat. Laurie, you tell him to disappear into the shadows and meet us just beyond the second street west of here. Tell him to pretend to be a rat if any human sees him. . . ."

Laurie was already talking, and Tweedlioop was climbing down my clothing even as I turned. In the shadowy city night, he did look rather like a large rat as he skittered off to the south. I almost called after him, afraid he'd misunderstood the directions. But by then the man across the street had crossed over and was coming straight toward us. I suppressed the urge and tried to act as if nothing had happened. It was one of the hardest acts I'd ever put on.

He was tall and lanky and dressed so his features were vague. "Out for a stroll?" he asked quietly.

"Yes, sir," I said. *Why did I say "Sir"?*

He nodded. "Not a bad night for it." He paused. "Where's your alien friend?"

My mouth went utterly dry—perhaps just as well, since it kept me from saying anything. Danni managed to sound remarkably calm. "What are you talking about?"

"I think you know, Ms. O'Millian," said the stranger. "Now that we've established who you are, I suppose you'll want to know who I am." He flashed a small leather folder containing a metal badge and a card. Danni barely glanced at it.

"Okay," she said. "I'm convinced. But I repeat: what are you talking about? You know as well as I that he's being held under very tight security. Do you need us to tell you where?"

Irritation flickered in the agent's face. "He's dis—" He stopped himself and started over. "I'm supposed to keep an eye on you and watch for odd comings and goings. Wouldn't you say a stroll at this hour qualifies?" He stood a little taller. "I'm afraid I'm going to have to search all of you."

He actually frisked us. He scowled when he couldn't find anything, but he let us go. We walked a couple of blocks. Maddeningly, I couldn't get Danni to put on any speed, even though she glanced back as often as I did. Before long, though, it became clear that we were headed in a roundabout way for the spot where she'd told Tweed-lioop to meet us. I was afraid of what we'd find—or not find—when we got there. But muggers seldom bother rats, for the same reason I jumped when I thought I saw one in a doorway.

It was him. And a cab happened by mere seconds later, just as I finished stuffing Tweedlioop back into my coat, and Danni made sure we got that one. The driver was every inch the legendary New York cabbie, and he whisked us up Third Avenue in a time quite competitive with the subway. It was one of the best amusement-park rides I'd ever been on.

The address Danni gave him was not Lois's, and after the cab dropped us off we had a brisk walk of two short blocks and most of a long one before we reached her doorway. "Wait here," Danni said in the vestibule. "I'll go up and get back down as fast as I can." She pressed Lois's button, identified herself, and Lois buzzed her in. Laurie and Tweedlioop and I stood and fidgeted.

Danni was back in five minutes, keys in hand. "Even faster than I'd hoped," she said. "Sometimes Lois really comes through in a pinch. She's phoning ahead so the garage attendant will expect us."

Todd's Garage was across the street. The attendant, a slender young black man who seemed surprisingly cheerful for this hour, was indeed expecting us. He looked us over, compared Danni's keys with the ones in his locked cabinet, then disappeared through a door. He was back in three minutes with an immaculate yellow sedan that looked wholly appropriate to Lois Sendelman. Danni slipped him a couple of bills and we all piled into the front seat, she at the helm.

We pulled out into the night and threaded our way through residential and commercial streets for a few blocks. Then we swung north, if I read the sign correctly, on F.D.R. Drive. It was a nice high-speed highway that whisked us smoothly north along the East River. The car purred like the proverbial kitten; its interior smelled new. We spun past a couple of big, picturesquely lit bridges, and soon crossed one—the George Washington, I think. Then we had a long ride north on the Palisades Parkway, seemingly leaving the city and traveling through woods. "No more stops or crowds for a while," Danni said. "Why don't you take Tweedlioop out for some air?"

I did, and for most of the trip he sat on Laurie's lap and she stroked him. "That was scary back there," I said finally. "Why didn't we just take that first cab when we had the chance?"

"Because," said Danni, "I was reasonably sure we were under surveillance and it wouldn't be long before somebody noticed Tweedlioop was missing. I was betting I knew who Mr. Sinister was, and that if we could *show* him we didn't have Tweedlioop, they'd take their suspicions elsewhere for a while. But not for long, I'm afraid. I wish I dared speed."

Silence settled over us; Danni concentrated fiercely on her driving. I could sense her frustration, but only because I knew her. The road was big, divided, and well maintained, and at the moment carried little traffic. She could have opened the car up and got us wherever we were going much faster—if we got there at all. But she dared not attract trooperish attention, as long as it appeared we weren't being followed, so she held strictly to the speed limit and the middle of the lane.

"Decision time," she said a little later. She kept glancing at the rearview mirrors. "I was going to turn off and make a phone call, but I don't know if we dare. That pair of headlights has been with us for quite a while." She drove on silently for a minute or so. We came to a traffic circle that I figured must be where she'd planned to get off, but instead of doing so she went all the way around the circle. Twice.

So did the headlights.

"That's good enough for me," she said tensely, leaving the circle still on the Parkway. "I don't think we need to call. They already know." She went silent again. She was stretching the limit a bit now, but still not too much. I kept my mouth shut, letting her think. The next few miles went through a huge park—the one she'd told me about, I guessed—where big rounded hills loomed black against a sky lit by a gibbous moon in the west. At one point our headlights caught the eyes of four deer beside the road, and I began to realize how right she'd been about the country near New York.

"They know it's us," she said suddenly, letting her latest thoughts out. "First they knew Tweedlioop was gone—we already knew that—and even though that spook found us clean, he'd be suspicious. They obviously knew where we were by the time we left, so we don't need to tell them where to look for the note. I think they found it a long time ago. So why are they hanging back there now?"

Our road swung down a long slope toward a suspension bridge strung between imposingly rugged hills and lit up like a Christmas tree. "Maybe they want us to lead them to your rendezvous point," I suggested. We spun around another traffic circle, past the end of the bridge, and exited onto a road that crawled briefly through a little hamlet with side streets and taverns and stores.

"That's all I thought of, too," Danni said, "but it doesn't make sense. The only reason they'd care about the pickup point is to try to get Tweedlioop back before the Ambassador does." The road opened up again, and we climbed a long northward slope with occasional glimpses of the river far below. Danni was riding the accelerator a little harder with each passing minute. The headlights stayed in view behind us, but made no apparent attempt to overtake, suggesting that they did not belong to an ordinary police car—and that if they were after Tweedlioop, they didn't want us to know it yet. "I suppose it's *possible* it's just coincidence," she said, "and it's not them at all. But following us around that circle looks mighty suspicious."

"Maybe they don't want to scare us into doing anything rash," I said. "If we crashed and Tweedlioop was killed, they'd lose everything."

"Yeah," said Laurie. "They know we're going to have to get out of the car. They probably figure that's the safest time to grab him."

"Hm-m-m," said Danni. "Might be something to that. . . . And as long as I'm driving fairly normally, they figure they've got it made." She watched the mirrors for several seconds. The road had been straight and open coming up the mountain, and our pursuer—if he was indeed such—

had allowed himself the luxury of dropping fairly far back, perhaps to reduce our suspicions. Near the crest, the road swung broadly but decisively left, and the instant the headlights disappeared around the bend Danni floored the accelerator and downshifted. We squealed but hugged the road as we catapulted forward. We must have surged up to a hundred or so, and she didn't let up a bit more than curves demanded for the rest of the trip. A few seconds of that, after the false sense of security she'd encouraged with her conservative driving before, was enough to get us a good hefty lead before the other car reappeared.

We dipped down between two of Danni's mountains and careened around another couple of curves, again losing the headlights. And at the end, during one of those moments of isolation, she slammed on the brakes and whipped the car off the road as it slowed, keeping the maneuver just slow enough to avoid flipping. I barely had time to see that we were in a roadside parking area with a forbidding cliff rising to the left and a long valley stretching down to the Hudson before she killed the lights. I sucked in breath as I saw we weren't going to be able to stop before the edge, and we were barely going to fit, if we fit at all, between two boulders. As the pursuing headlights roared around the last curve, rock scraped metal on both sides, we slowed with an additional jerk, and the bottom dropped out of our world as we tilted and fell. . . .

But not far. As the lights disappeared around yet another bend, I heard a great crunching of branches as trees and shrubs broke our fall. Then there was silence; somewhere in there Danni had already killed the engine. "Sorry, Lois," she muttered as she opened her seat belt and door. "I'll get it fixed or buy you a new one or something." To us: "Everybody out. It won't take them long to realize we're off the road."

None of us was hurt. The nose of the car was angled steeply downward, but the doors opened without too much trouble and it was only a short drop to crumpled shrubbery and assorted litter. "Sorry if I scared you," said Danni, already scrambling along the bank to the north, "but I knew it wouldn't be too bad here, and I didn't see any other way. Hope nobody's allergic to poison ivy." Staying below the rim, marked by those boulders and occasionally a stretch of guardrail, she gestured ahead at the looming cliff. "Butter Hill," she said. "We'll go up over that and on out to Storm King. That's what we described to the Ambassador. It's not as bad as it looks."

We followed, Tweedlioop clinging to Laurie's shoulder. Beyond the parking area there was a trail of sorts heading into the woods, though how Danni knew it was there—other than having used it before—was beyond me. After a little while it opened up and clambered up steepish boulders and ledges. Enough moonlight reached the rocks to make out an occasional paint blaze; I could only assume the whole trail was so marked. And that made me wonder. . . . "If this is a marked trail," I panted, "won't it make it awfully easy to follow?"

"Only," said Danni without slowing down or looking back, "if our pursuer happens to be a hiker who knows this area. There's no sign at the parking area; it just looks like an overlook with a few picnic tables. If you don't know the trail's here—and not many do—you won't notice it even in daylight. Besides, we have no choice. Any other route would be much too slow—and dangerous, in this light."

Feeling only trivially less pursued, I struggled onward.

From some of the open places, I saw the massive shoulder of Butter Hill, now ahead and to the right. Danni was right that the trail wasn't as bad as going straight up the cliffs, but it was plenty rough to do at night. For a while, stretches of dark woods alternated with rocky climbs, some of them pretty steep, and we just had to pick our way as best we could without unduly compromising safety. As we approached the summit of Butter Hill, the trail followed some ledges with enough exposure to be more than a little scary in semidarkness. I could see that in daylight the views would be spectacular.

The trail, except for a couple of brief spots, got much easier beyond the summit. Only a shallow saddle separated Butter Hill from Storm King, and the trail there was mostly easy walking through open woods with grassy floors and occasional stands of mountain laurel. We came over a little knob into one grassy glade and were startled by a crashing commotion as two equally startled deer bounded for cover.

The trail finally swung out onto an open place with an impressive view up the river; a long bridge linked two jewel-like clusters of city lights. Danni slowed down. "Have to be careful here," she said. "The trail goes on down to another road, but we don't want to do that. We have to leave the trail. . . . Ah, here."

The home stretch was a tricky bushwhack down through a thicket, with scratchy branches and treacherous ledges to watch out for. But soon we emerged into a place that I could tell, even in this light, was really something. Behind us were the trees from which we had just emerged. A few yards ahead, it seemed, was the edge of the world, with a sheer drop to the river valley a thousand feet below.

Between was a large expanse of gentle slope, mostly open, with beds of tall grass punctuated by rocky ledges. We could be easily seen there, and there were any number of places where the manouverable little shuttles of the chucks could presumably land.

"And now we wait," said Danni. "Let's make ourselves comfortable."

I wasn't sure I could do that, but I was more than ready for a rest. Now that we were stationary and exposed to breezes, we could notice how chilly it was. I was glad Danni had insisted on the jackets and the blanket, which she had carried on the trail like a cape fastened around her with a big safety pin. Now she took it off and sought out a grassy, benchlike ledge where we could all sit, backed by a boulder we could lean against. We all sat down, huddled together, the blanket wrapped around us. At first the rock felt cold, but that passed.

Laurie asked Tweedlioop, "Do you think they'll find us here?" He warbled quite a while, and she told us, "He thinks they can; the description was clear enough. But he's not sure who will come. The Ambassador may try it himself—or he may assume they'll follow him and lead them off in a wrong direction."

"But then who—" I began.

"Remember when General Goodmill asked if there were other chucks and the Ambassador didn't answer? Well, there are. If the Ambassador decides to play decoy, he'll call another shuttle on a closed channel to come and get Tweedlioop."

"Good," said Danni. "That will improve our chances, but it's still touch and go. The government will anticipate that possibility, too, and if the Ambassador leads them one way and we lead them another, they'll have somebody following both—they already do, in fact, as we well know. It's going to be tense, whatever happens."

Nobody spoke for a while. The moon had set, or at least gone behind the hills. The mountains no longer stood out so clearly on either side of the river. Wondrous swarms of stars were emerging from the darkening sky, and I felt closer to them than ever before. I had a friend, after all, who was trying to get back to one of them. . . .

"Tweedlioop," I said softly, "you told us once you were a little afraid to go back. Can you tell us why now?"

Laurie had to help to get my question through to him, and even afterward he was silent for a couple of seconds before he answered. But only a couple of seconds, and in some hard-to-define way he seemed calmer than ever before—as if his whole experience on Earth had had some maturing effect on him.

Which, of course, was exactly what it was intended to do.

"You know part of it," he said through Laurie. "My stay here was supposed to help me learn, and it was also a test—which I failed, at least partially. I was not supposed to come into contact with any of you, and I didn't want to face my teachers after I was unable to survive any other way. But I realize now that sometimes failing is less important than what you learn from it, and I'll bet my teachers understood that long before I did. In any case, I have to face the music. A Ruler is accountable for everything he does—and I am a Ruler-in-Reserve."

He paused, then haltingly added, "There was one more thing. I was playing around in a way I shouldn't have been when the shuttle malfunctioned, and I imagined that the crash was my fault. But I was a child then, and I see now that that was silly. I'm ready now. I hope I get the chance."

Again we were all quiet, our minds full. Then Danni said, "Suppose we'd stayed in New York and let them play out their game. Do you think the Ambassador would have given in and given them what they wanted to get you back?"

"No," said Tweedlioop, without hesitation.

"Would your people have used force against us?"

"No. Our nonviolence runs deeper than most humans seem able to grasp. So does our noninterference. They would have tried a great many other things to get me back, and probably one of them would have worked. But if none did, they would leave me—with regret, but they would leave me."

We chewed on that for a while. I think exhaustion was beginning to catch up with all of us. But there was one more thing I had to ask him, though I was a little afraid of the answer. "If you get home and someday become Ruler, how will you remember Earth?"

"With mixed feelings," he said. "My experience with your government has been distressing, of course—though probably not surprising for a planet at this stage in its history. But what I'll remember most will be you three— and because of you, some of my memories will be fond ones. With people like you here, there's hope for Earth."

None of us could think of anything to say after that. I stared at the sky, profoundly moved. After a while I thought of one more question: was it possible that Tweedlioop, as Ruler, reflecting on his own experience, would decide that contact with young races did *not* have to be absolutely avoided? That someday, maybe, we would even see him again?

But I couldn't ask him that. I forced the thought from my mind and let myself drift down toward a much-needed sleep, as an owl hooted somewhere below. When consciousness was almost gone, I roused myself enough to ask, "Shouldn't somebody stay awake and stand guard? What if they bring dogs?"

"I don't think they will before morning," said Danni. "And if they do, I don't know a thing we can do about it. We've done all we can." She reached over and touched my hand. "Go to sleep, Bill."

Somehow, eventually, I did. But it took a long time, and even then I was pursued through my dreams by wolves and politicians, and sometimes it was hard to tell which were which. But finally came real rest, and of that I remember nothing.

I woke to a persistent, excited chattering from Tweedlioop—a ratchety noise, the most genuinely squirrel-like I had ever heard from him.

He was out of the blanket and dancing around on the nearest ledge, gesturing wildly like that time in Alaska when he had first tried to tell me who he was. I couldn't see what had him so excited, but the feeling of *déjà vu* persisted. The eastern sky had paled considerably; the air was crystal-clear and the mountains looked like velvet with the first touches of fall color. A white blanket of fog lay on the river. The hills were different, on close inspection, and I could see a small town across the river, but the overall feel of things drew my mind right back to Alaska. Even the little green Cessna that was purring contentedly down the middle of the valley, its pilot likely out to catch the dawn . . .

Danni and Laurie were still asleep, but Laurie woke suddenly, watching Tweedlioop and listening intently. "They're coming!" she said, jumping up so abruptly that she pulled the blanket off us and woke Danni, too.

I still couldn't see or hear anything, but when the Cessna had vanished from sight and earshot, it finally hit me. What remained was not silence, but a soft pink rushing noise that seemed to be circling us. Following the sound and Tweedlioop's pointing, I finally found it—and was astonished at how close it already was.

I had never seen a chuck shuttle in flight before, and I was quite unprepared for how *quiet* it was. It looked just like the ones I'd seen, except it was sky-blue and almost invisible. Its lack of wings or rotors seemed incongruous— it obviously worked on something other than aerodynamic principles—and yet it seemed in fuller control of its motions than any human-built aircraft. It was circling very slowly, hardly more than a hundred feet above us. . . .

Danni and I stood up, too, and joined Tweedlioop and Laurie in jumping around and waving to attract its attention. Danni picked up our blanket and brandished it like a *torero*'s cape.

And the little blue shuttle swerved, still purring ever so gently, and began to settle toward us.

Even as it did so, I heard the ungainly *chop-chop-chop* of a fair-sized helicopter, still fairly distant but approaching fast. I spotted it coming up the river, already almost to Crows Nest, the next peak south, and my heart tried to climb up my gullet. Of course it *might* be on unrelated business, its appearance there and then mere coincidence.

But I knew better, really. I knew that what was really happening was just what Danni had predicted. Giannelli and the Ambassador were racing after Tweedlioop, and the race was about to end.

Even though we already knew we'd been spotted, we redoubled our efforts to call the alien shuttle in. By now its tiny purr was completely swamped by the chopper, even as it settled onto a flat rock fifty feet from us. As we ran toward it, its color changed smoothly from sky-blue to a subtly mottled gray like the rock on which it sat. Only when we were right beside it could I hear it again; its "engine" was still running. I also saw then that it wasn't really sitting on the rock, but suspended, quite motionless, two or three inches above.

As we arrived, a two-by-three-foot oval of wall disappeared in front of us. Inside were two chucks—not the Ambassador and his Silent Partner, but two strangers of the different "gender" who looked like orange-furred wolverines. But Tweedlioop recognized them, and he and they chattered vigorously at each other as they lifted him aboard. He turned and said something to us, but Laurie couldn't hear him well enough to understand it. Giannelli's copter was too close by then. We barely had time to wave before the missing oval of hull reappeared and we were watching the shuttle, again featureless, lifting rapidly skyward and already returning to blue.

And then it disappeared.

Completely.

"Good-bye, little fella," Danni whispered. I could hear her because the copter had throttled way back as it settled onto another nearby rocky platform.

"Be a good Ruler," Laurie added. Tears were streaming

down both their faces—and I wasn't sure my own eyes were as dry as they could have been.

Behind us, the copter had killed its engine and its noise was dying as its rotor clattered to a halt. I heard a hatch thrown open and footsteps running across the rock toward us.

It was Giannelli himself, and he was livid. "Do you realize what you've done?" he raged. "We had a chance no one's ever had before and may never have again, and you threw it away! We *needed* what they could have given us! You know that, Nordstrom! And they would have given in, in time. . . . But you had to meddle, and now we have *nothing.*"

He stood there, shaking with his fury, and I felt sorry for him. I had wanted what he wanted, too—but not enough to throw away every other consideration that was important to me. "I'm sorry, Mr. President," I said quietly, facing him with a surprising calm. "But I really don't think they would have. And we don't have 'nothing.' Some of us have our integrity, peace of mind, self-respect. All of us have the knowledge that *it can be done.* If we don't do it, knowing that, we have no one to blame but ourselves. But I think we will."

"And if we do," said Laurie, "it will be better if we do it for ourselves."

"Pah!" the President spat. "Do you think empty platitudes will impress the U.N., or the courts, or the American people? You're coming back with me, and—"

"I think not, Mr. President," Danni interrupted. "On what grounds? Treason? Where was the declaration of war? Where was even an executive order forbidding us to do what we did? Or any evidence that returning Tweedlioop has hurt us or keeping him could have helped us?" She laughed, and I could see that that bothered him more than anything either of us had said yet. "The car was legally borrowed, and I'll be paying for any damage. We'll even return the blanket we borrowed from the hotel. I haven't checked out yet, you know." Her tone became serious again. "No, Mr. President, there's too little law and too little precedent for this. You can all thrash out among yourselves what you *should* have done. Then you can come after us if you still want to and can find a legal pretext—but somehow I doubt you're going to want the publicity."

"But you might want some other kind," I said, thinking of that U.N. videotape and the wrecked shuttle somebody still had in storage. "Think about it."

He ignored me. "Maybe," said Danni, "you'll be better prepared next time—but this time it will all be *ex post facto*. So while you talk it over, we'll walk out of here the same way we walked in."

Giannelli glared at her for a long time, breathing heavily. Finally he grated, "Okay, I'll let you go for now. But don't think you've heard the last of this. At the very least, I can see that you'll never practice law again. And *you*" —he glowered at me—"will never work on a government contract again."

He stamped back to the helicopter, climbed aboard, and slammed the hatch. The engine roared to life, and we watched it lift off and head back toward the city.

When we could hear again, I asked Danni, "Can he really do that?"

"Probably," she said. "But we can both find other work. Wasn't it worth it?"

I thought about it for just a few seconds and found that I had no doubts at all. "Yes," I said. Maybe, I thought, Giannelli would even come to his senses and see how to use the Tweedlioop Incident to build a psychological fire under humankind that would drive us outward to our full potential.

But I wasn't going to stake my personal future on it.

The sun was creeping over the hills on the other side of the river. I saw its glint on Danni's spun-copper hair and remembered something I had thought once on a beach in Florida. Maybe someday, I told myself, I *would* take artistic photographs of it.

One way or another, we would build new lives. I had no doubt of that.

And we just might do it together.

Our careers very probably shattered, but very much at peace with ourselves, we gathered our things and started slowly out. Before long, I hoped, we would be back in Naples.

And this time, I promised myself, I *would* take Laurie out on that pier, and we would spend all the time we wanted feeding the pelicans.

THE END

THE BEST IN FANTASY